WHEN THE
SNOW FLIES

Other Available Books by Laurie Alice Eakes:

Family Guardian

WHEN THE
SNOW FLIES

•

Laurie Alice Eakes

AVALON BOOKS
NEW YORK

Published by Thomas Bouregy & Co., Inc.
160 Madison Avenue, New York, NY 10016

Library of Congress Cataloging-in-Publication Data

Eakes, Laurie Alice.
   When the snow flies / Laurie Alice Eakes.
      p. cm.
   ISBN 978-0-8034-7776-6
   1. Women physicians—Fiction.   2. Virginia—History—
19th century—Fiction.   I. Title.
   PS3605.A377W47 2010
   813'.6—dc22

                                             2010006231

PRINTED IN THE UNITED STATES OF AMERICA
ON ACID-FREE PAPER
BY HADDON CRAFTSMEN, BLOOMSBURG, PENNSYLVANIA

To my elder sister,
who doesn't let her blindness stop
her from doing amazing things.

Chapter One

No one met Audrey Vanderleyden at the train. A wizened old man with hair like mountain mist popped out of the station, spoke with the conductor for a moment, then darted into the clapboard building without so much as glancing Audrey's way.

The train pulled out of the station. Audrey remained on the platform amidst a collection of trunks and valises until the locomotive's last whistle died away in the valley, and pine resin scent from the planks beneath her feet overcame the stench of coal smoke. Still no one came to meet her, neither a porter from the hotel nor Dr. Hornsby, with whom she had an appointment in an hour, according to the watch pinned to her black lapel.

She left all but one of her bags behind and marched toward the station. Her black muslin skirts hampered her brisk stride, and she kicked them out of her way with each step. When she reached the door, she yanked it open, took one step into the hot, still air, and stopped to look around.

In one corner, the telegraph machine clattered. A diminutive operator sat beside it with his booted feet propped up on the desk—on which lay a slip of yellow paper with the words addressed to Dr. Hornsby printed in bold, black letters.

DR. A. S. VANDERLEYDEN ARRIVE AFTERNOON TRAIN TUESDAY STOP MEET HOUR LATER STOP

The message for the hotel was similar and requested that a conveyance meet her at the train.

"You didn't deliver my messages." She used the same tone she too often had to use on nurses who failed to carry out her orders for a patient's care.

As did those nurses, the old man jumped. His heels hit the wooden floor with a resounding thud, and he sprang to his feet. "Ma'am? I . . . uh . . . don't know what y'all are talkin' about."

"These." Audrey stalked forward and snatched up the messages. "They should have been delivered two days ago."

The telegrapher shrugged. "No sense in it."

"No sense—" Audrey paused to take a deep breath and count to ten before her voice shifted from mellow alto to shrill soprano. "And why, pray tell, is there no use delivering messages I paid Western Union to deliver?"

"Thought it was a mistake."

Audrey set her jaw and tried to meet his gaze while she waited for him to explain.

He didn't look her in the eye, an easy evasion, as she stood half a head taller than him. "Well, gosh, ma'am." He rubbed his bluish nose.

Audrey caught a whiff of smoked fish on his breath, and her stomach roiled.

"We all heard Dr. Vanderleyden died 'bout three months ago," the telegrapher explained.

Audrey tensed inside her plain black mourning suit. A wave of sadness calmed her racing pulse.

"Dr. Adam Stephen Vanderleyden did pass away fourteen

weeks ago. I—" She gripped her leather bag more tightly in one lace-gloved hand. "I'm Dr. Audrey Sinclair Vanderleyden, his wife—widow."

Even before she stopped speaking, he was shaking his head, sending the wispy gray hair floating up like fluff from a dandelion. She half expected him to deny her claim. Instead, he murmured, "Quarter century back, I thought the War Between the States was the worst thing I'd ever witnessed. But a lady doctor's about got that beat."

"Indeed." Audrey's nostrils flared. "Well, sir, whether you like it or not, I am a fully qualified physician, and I am taking over the practice my late husband and I purchased from Dr. William Hornsby."

"Humph." The telegrapher turned his back on her. "We'll see about that."

"We certainly will." Audrey spun on the heels of her high-buttoned shoes and strode out of the station.

With the sun pouring over her like molten bronze, she stood on the platform beside her luggage and waited for her heart to return to a normal rate and her breathing to calm. When she met Dr. Hornsby, she needed to be cool, composed, and every bit as professional as a male doctor meeting the man from whom he had purchased a practice. No matter what he said, no matter how he reacted to learning she was a female, she must not demonstrate any of the emotions that prejudiced men against women in the professions—hysteria, temper, tears. She must demonstrate no emotion at all.

Since the station, platform, and surrounding area appeared devoid of life, save for a handful of black-and-white cows in a nearby field, Audrey figured no one would steal her luggage. Leaving it on the platform, she headed for the business district in town.

She walked, though she wanted to run. Heat, fatigue, and her stiff mourning clothes hampered her progress. The medical bag, full of shiny new instruments, grew heavier with each yard, and her mouth felt as if she'd been chewing on papyrus scrolls excavated from the deserts of Egypt. At least she wasn't wearing a corset, and half a mile wasn't far. She'd walked six times that distance every day in Paris, and nearly that much in New York what felt like a lifetime ago.

A carefree lifetime ago.

Shaking off the thought, she squared her narrow shoulders and adjusted the short veil on her hat to allow the light breeze to touch her face. Without the black netting obscuring her vision, the little town appeared brighter and more alive, with spills of roses and begonias in front of the shops. A few horses and carriages trundled up the streets, and people strolled in and out of the businesses.

She spotted the hotel on the corner of Main and Church Streets and stepped from the hot sunlight outside to what seemed like cool twilight inside. The desk clerk arched his eyebrows but rose and gave her a welcoming smile.

"Dr. Vanderleyden." Audrey announced herself.

The clerk's dark brows nearly disappeared into his hairline. "Doctor?"

She chose to ignore his astonishment. "You were supposed to receive a telegram announcing my arrival and requesting conveyance from the train."

"We received no communication, ma'am . . . er . . . Doctor." He scrambled for the registration book. "But we have rooms. Bath or no bath? With is four bits extra."

"That will be suitable."

If more expensive than she could truly afford. But she needed the luxury right now.

She paid for the first two nights, hoping she could find less expensive accommodations in that amount of time. The clerk agreed to have someone fetch her luggage, and she stepped back into the heat of the July afternoon. The clerk had assured her she couldn't miss Doc Hornsby's surgery two blocks away.

Half a block away, she passed the drugstore. She had another twenty minutes until the time she had set to meet with the doctor, unbeknownst to him, and a cold sarsaparilla sounded good. She hadn't had anything to drink since leaving Union Station in Washington, D.C., two hours earlier. Inside, new electric ceiling fans churned overhead, creating the illusion of coolness.

She half turned toward the open wood-and-glass door and caught sight of customers at the counter chatting with one another. She didn't want to be stared at and forced into introducing herself to anyone before meeting Dr. Hornsby.

She quickened her pace, taking longer and swifter strides until she arrived at the office, breathless and dewy.

The door stood open. A light breeze wafted from the door to the open window, stirring air scented with alcohol and iodine. Audrey's nostrils flared. Her stomach churned. She set down her valise and grasped the door frame.

"Do sit down before you fall down, ma'am." The voice was clear, light, and flavored with amusement and the South.

Audrey glanced toward the speaker. She was probably a decade older than Audrey, placing her in her mid-thirties. A saucy yellow hat perched atop her gold-veined hair, and her sea-blue eyes twinkled in a face with a bone structure that would make her beautiful all her life.

"Doc will be out in a minute," she continued. "He's stitching up my brother's hand."

Beyond a white door, low voices murmured, one complaining, the other chuckling.

Rather unkind of a doctor to chuckle while setting stitches, thought Audrey.

"Nothing serious, I hope." Audrey hefted her bag and stepped into the waiting room that could have passed for a plantation parlor. "How many stitches? What did he cut it wi—I'm so sorry." Her face heated from more than her dash to the office. "It's none of my business, of course. It's just that—" She glanced down at her bag. "I'm a doctor."

"You're a what, ma'am?"

"A doctor. A physician." Audrey held out her hand. "Dr. Audrey Sinclair Vanderleyden."

"*You're* Dr. A. S. Vanderleyden?" The woman's eyes widened, and she clasped her hands over her plump middle.

No, not plump. She was expecting. And rather far along for being out in public. Six or seven months, thought Audrey.

"Yes." She kept her response simple.

"But I thought . . . We all thought . . ." The woman's voice trailed off, her face puckering with confusion. "Doc never said a female doctor was coming to take over his practice. In fact, we thought there was an accident. . . ."

"Two doctors were to take over his practice." Audrey clasped her hands at her waist and took several long, deep breaths. "My husband carried out the negotiations. But when he . . . died, I made no attempt to break the contract."

She had nowhere else to go if she wanted to practice medicine sooner rather than later. Much later, probably.

"Well, I'm sure you can make everything clear with Doc," the woman said in a brusque way that indicated she was sure of nothing of the kind. "He's sober today, and that means—" Her gloved hand flew to her mouth, then she heaved herself to her feet and held out that hand. "I am forgetting my manners. I'm Corinne Chapman."

They touched fingertips, Audrey's encased in black lace, Corinne's in snowy kid.

"Apparently the telegraph operator never delivered my telegram," Audrey said.

"It wouldn't have mattered if he had." Corinne glanced toward a door on the far side of the room.

More grumbling and chuckling reverberated through the panels in desperate need of dusting.

"My brother needed help quickly," Corinne chattered on. "I told him not to take up carving, but he insisted that he needed a hobby. He does, but the blood! I can't abide blood at the best of times, you understand."

"Yes, I do understand." Audrey felt her knees weakening, and she dropped onto the nearest chair, an oversized relic with a seat wide enough to accommodate a lady in the bell hoops of thirty years ago. "I'll simply stay here and wait for the doctor to finish."

And worry about his reaction to the fact that she was Audrey Sinclair, not Adam Stephen, Vanderleyden.

"He shouldn't be much longer," Corinne said. "In fact, I hear them coming now."

Indeed, two pairs of footfalls sounded beyond the inner door. It opened, and Audrey felt momentarily breathless.

The first man to appear filled the doorway with his height and shoulder width. He had caramel-colored hair streaked with gold, and eyes the color of the sea on a clear day—a deep, fathomless blue. His features were strong and saved from too much perfection by a bump below the bridge of his nose, as though he'd broken it at some point in time. His smile was wide enough, bright enough, and warm enough to melt an iceberg.

He didn't so much as glance in Audrey's direction. His sister, the relationship obvious from their resemblance, sprang up and hugged him, scolding him with comments like, "I hope it hurt. You deserve it for being so silly. If you ever . . . But there's no blood. . . ."

Audrey remained motionless in her chair, knowing her reaction to the man was completely wrong for a widow of only three and a half months. Loyalty, if not a broken heart, should have kept her from feeling a thrill of appreciation run through her.

"But I am forgetting my manners," Corinne exclaimed again. "Nathan, there's someone here you should meet. And Doc, too, of course. Mrs. Vanderleyden."

"Doctor," Audrey said reflexively.

"Of course, how thoughtless of me." Corinne clasped her brother's intact right hand and stretched it toward Audrey.

Audrey sprang to her feet and grasped it, a polite greeting caught in her throat when she realized Nathan's beautiful blue eyes could see absolutely nothing.

"What's this about a doctor here?" A short, stocky man with a red nose and yellowish skin pushed past Nathan to glare at Audrey. "You're not Dr. Vanderleyden. He's dead."

"Yes, Dr. Adam Stephen Vanderleyden is dead," Audrey said for what felt like the hundredth time that day. "I am Dr. Audrey Sinclair Vanderleyden."

"She sounds prettier than you, Doc." Nathan grinned.

"Humph." Doc narrowed his muddy brown eyes. "Pretty is as pretty does, and nothing pretty does doctoring."

Audrey pulled herself to her full five feet four inches, half a head shorter than the doctor. "I am a fully qualified medical doctor with degrees from Vassar and the Sorbonne. I have practiced in New York City hospitals for a year, and I have a contract that says I have paid you money to purchase and take over this practice on Monday, August 2."

Silence fell. Doc opened and closed his mouth like a gasping fish. Nathan looked bemused or a little sad. A carriage pulled up outside, and Corinne let out a nervous titter.

"The carriage is here," she said overly cheerfully. "We'd best be on our way and let Mrs. Vanderleyden and Doc discuss business in private."

"I believe that's Dr. Vanderleyden, Corinne." Nathan grinned in Audrey's direction.

"No woman is a doctor," Doc thundered. "It's unnatural. It's obscene." He took a step closer to Audrey, close enough for his hot breath to pour over her face with more force than the breeze from the window. "It's— It's— What's wrong with you, woman?"

Audrey held her hand in front of her face to block the spirituous fumes wafting from the doctor. The odor made her feel ill and light-headed, and she feared she must have gone pale.

"You smell of liquor," Audrey said. "I don't care for the smell."

"I don't either." Corinne tugged on Nathan's arm. "Come along. We shouldn't keep the horses standing in this heat."

"No, we shouldn't, but—" Nathan drew his golden brown brows together. "Doc, I only interfere here because I've known you all my life. So I'm asking you if Dr. Vanderleyden is right. Do you have a contract with her?"

"I do not." Doc's feet stomped the wooden floorboards as he turned to face Nathan. "I have a contract with Dr. A. S. Vanderleyden. Three months ago, I received word that he was killed in a riding accident."

"Boating." Audrey reached out to find something to hang on to. She found nothing.

"Mrs. . . . um . . . Dr. Vanderleyden?" Corinne was gazing at Audrey from beneath gold-tipped lashes. "Perhaps you should sit down. You look faint."

"Which is just one of the thousand reasons why no woman can be a doctor," Doc said. "And I am under no contractual obligation to turn my practice over to this fraud. The contract—"

"Was signed by both my late husband and me," Audrey broke in. "If you will get your copy, you will notice that it has two signatures on the purchaser's side."

"I don't have it." Doc stuck out his nonexistent chin.

"Why not?" Nathan asked.

"Really, brother, this is none of our concern," Corinne said, tugging harder on his arm.

He removed his arm from her hold. "Neither of them has asked us to leave, Corinne, and I'm interested in seeing this resolved."

"Are you an attorney?" Audrey thought she would hire him on the spot if he were.

He gave her a smile that carried sadness from the depths of his blue eyes. "No, ma'am, I was a doctor too."

"I see—" She pressed the back of her hand to her lips. With an effort, she refrained from asking him what had happened to make him lose his sight. Instead, she reached for her medical bag to withdraw her own copy of the contract. "Here is my copy. As you will notice, Dr. Hornsby, there are two signatures on the side of the purchaser."

"A forgery." He didn't even glance at the document. "You doctored it. Ha."

"I'll go tell James to drive around the block again." Corinne scuttled down the steps, pulling her shawl over her bulging middle.

"Then your copy will only have one signature," Nathan pointed out. "Why not fetch it?"

"I don't need to." Doc stomped toward the inner door. "I know what I saw." The door slammed behind him.

"I knew I'd face some opposition." Audrey blinked to clear her swimming vision. She wasn't crying; she was having a difficult time focusing. "But a contract is a— But don't let me hold you up, Dr. . . . ."

"Maxwell." He held out his hand to her, of his own accord this time. "Nathan Maxwell, but it's just Mister. I'm not a doctor any longer."

Audrey took his hand, admiring the long, strong fingers and feeling their warm clasp. "Once a doctor, always—"

Glass shattered on the other side of the door. An animal-like growl accompanied the crash.

Audrey sprinted across the waiting room and yanked open

the door. Doc stood in the center of the examining room with a glass of amber liquid in one hand. A splintered bottle lay at the foot of the far wall, more amber liquid spreading between the shards of glass. Fumes rose like miasma from a swamp.

Audrey staggered. Her back fell against Nathan Maxwell's chest, and his arms encircled her—stopping her from falling, holding her upright—with his hands against the front of her belly.

She cringed from the overly personal contact.

"Are you all right?" he asked.

"Yes, it's the fumes."

"Throw a bottle, Doc?" Nathan asked, as though the older man's show of temper was not uncommon.

"Get the contract. . . ." Doc muttered. "Well, I won't. I don't have it."

"Where . . . is it?" Audrey fought dizziness and nausea.

"I burned it when I heard Vanderleyden died."

"You burned it?" Nathan removed his hands from Audrey's waist but stayed close behind her. "Why'd you do a foolish thing like that?"

There was a silence, during which Doc drank from the glass.

"Then you owe me money." Audrey's voice didn't sound as strong as she would have liked. Her heart was beating far too quickly, and she was having a difficult time drawing in air. "You were paid—"

Her voice came from far away. Spots danced before her eyes, spots that grew larger and larger until complete blackness overtook over.

Within moments, she knew she'd fainted. "Heat," she mumbled, as strong arms lifted her.

"Put her on the table." Doc sounded impatient, angry. "Straight ahead."

"No, no," Audrey protested. "I'm all right. Just hungry."

Nathan laid her on the table, and she struggled to sit up.

He pressed a gentle but firm hand against her shoulder. "Lie still for a moment, Dr. Vanderleyden. Doc, open the window. This room reeks."

"Stupid female, thinking she can practice medicine," Doc muttered as he stomped across the room, "when a mere whiff of bourbon makes her faint."

"Oh, I don't think she's stupid in the least." Nathan's face tightened into grim lines. "*Unwise* is a better word for it."

"I'm a perfectly competent physician." Audrey managed a credible snapping tone. "Now, remove your hand from me so I may get up and go find an attorney."

"Dr. Vanderleyden," Nathan said, neither moving nor changing his expression, "an attorney might help you gain possession of this practice, but he can't change the fact that in another month or two, you won't be physically capable of practicing medicine."

"A month or two?" Doc snorted. "A minute or two is more like it."

"I have no idea what you're talking about." Audrey tried to sound as haughty as somebody could while lying on an examining table. Somebody who knew what he meant and feared she might faint again if her secret was exposed.

"Dr. Vanderleyden"—Nathan smiled with constraint—"even a blind man can tell you are at least four months along with child."

Chapter Two

The shoulder beneath Nathan's hand jerked back as though from a blow. He withdrew his hand and shoved it into his coat pocket. He stepped away from the examining table, an apology stuck on his tongue.

He didn't know for what to apologize—whether for diagnosing correctly or for diagnosing at all when he was no longer a doctor.

"That's really quite ridiculous, Dr. Maxwell." Audrey moved, and a scent of lilies of the valley swirled around the warm air. "I'm perfectly healthy when I've eaten."

"You look like a walking corpse," Doc grumbled. "But I have to admit that I agree with you. Nathan was a good doctor once, but he can't go around diagnosing now and without an examination."

Nathan steeled himself against the stab of pain from Doc's words. They were simply the truth, nothing to upset him.

"I had my hands on your waist when I caught you falling to the floor in a faint." Nathan enunciated each word with care. "You're not wearing a corset, and . . . The signs are obvious to the touch, if one knows what to look for. It's not as thorough an examination as . . . as I would have given you at one time to make such a diagnosis, true, but I stand by what I said. You can have Doc verify it, if you don't know yourself. But if you don't, I have to wonder about your capabilities as a physician."

He spoke to her as he would have a medical student at Johns Hopkins—crisply, clearly, and firmly. Perhaps also a little too sharply.

"I'm sorry." Hearing Corinne return to the waiting room, he swung away from her. "It's none of my concern."

"No, it's not." Audrey's tone held no rancor, merely a world of weariness. "And I don't want Doc to examine me."

For this Nathan didn't blame her. His old friend was no longer the caliber of physician he had been when he mentored Nathan through medical school and his first few years of practice. And Doc had only himself to blame for his downfall, something to which Nathan could relate.

His heart ached for the old man.

"It's quite true," Audrey continued in a melodic voice that sent an odd tingle racing through Nathan. "I am with child."

"Well, now," Doc said. "No expecting female, especially one without a husband, is going to practice medicine in this town."

"I have a husband," Audrey persisted. "I mean . . . I had a husband. Furthermore, I have a contract. You have to honor the contract or pay me back the money we gave you."

"Humph," Doc responded.

"Who's expecting?" Corinne spoke from close behind Nathan.

"Dr. Vanderleyden," he said. "She fainted, and I caught her."

"Well, then, I completely agree with Doc." Corinne bustled past Nathan, her skirt swishing. "My dear, Mrs.—Dr. Vanderleyden, we are happy to give you a ride down to the hotel. And if you need a lift to the train tomorrow, we can help you with that, as I'm certain we'll be in town again for something, and you'll want to return to your family."

"Thank you, but I'm not leaving until I have either the keys to this practice or my money back." As smooth as it was, like warm maple syrup, Audrey's voice held a thread of steel.

"You can't have either." Doc stalked across the room, his heavy footfalls making the floor vibrate. A drawer scraped open. Glass clinked.

"You drink in the middle of the afternoon?" Audrey sounded appalled.

Nathan cast her a grim smile. "He's quite sober for this time of day on account of my cutting open my hand."

The hand started to throb the minute he mentioned it. He'd been so wrapped up in the young woman's arrival and startling announcement, he hadn't paid much attention to his injury.

"Uppity females make me thirsty," Doc mumbled.

"I'm not being uppity by expecting you not to breach your contract," Audrey said. "Simply keep your word, or pay me back."

Doc's only response was a swallow and a gulp.

"We really need to be going." Corinne tugged on Nathan's good hand. "Dr. Vanderleyden, you do look unwell. Perhaps if you returned in the morning . . ."

"In the morning—"

"Wait." Nathan held up one hand, staying the young doctor's protest. "Will you let me talk to Doc alone? He'll likely be more responsive to another male doctor."

Audrey caught her breath, then let out a sigh. "All right. The smell of spirits is making me feel a bit ill."

"The air outside is fresher, if not cooler," Corinne said. "Come along."

Skirts whispered across the floor to the rhythm of two sets of light footfalls. The door closed.

"I can breathe again." Doc thumped the bottle he was holding onto a solid surface. "Can't abide females who think they have the brains to be doctors. It's all the fault of the Europeans. No decent university in this country lets them in."

"Actually," Nathan drawled, "Johns Hopkins just started admitting women."

"And you're not protesting?" Doc slurped again. "For shame."

"What right or reason do I have to protest?" Nathan shrugged. "Women are lawyers and journalists too. I don't know why they can't be doctors."

"They're too emotional, too delicate. Look at your sister. She was practically fainting at the sight of blood when she brought you in."

"I expect Dr. Vanderleyden doesn't faint at the sight of blood if she's made it through medical school." Nathan drummed the fingers of his good hand on his thigh. "Doc, you know you need to honor the contract or pay back the money. If she's a fully qualified physician, you won't win in court, and it'll cost you a lot of money. Besides, you're seventy-two years old. You should retire."

Not to mention the man should retire before he hurt someone by doctoring while under the influence.

"I intended to retire." The bottle thudded again. "Can't now."

Can't or *won't?* Nathan wondered.

"No female doctor practices on my patients."

Decisiveness. Determination. Two qualities Nathan hadn't heard in the older man's voice in two years. Because he was loyal to the few patients he had left? Nathan wouldn't have thought so, but maybe . . .

"Then pay her back the purchase money."

Even as he said it, Nathan suspected that Doc didn't have the money. For two years now, since Doc's wife of fifty years died, most folks had been traveling the ten miles or so to Winchester for medical care. Doc had probably needed the money for the practice to pay off debts.

"Were you to receive a percentage of the profits from the practice for a while?" Nathan asked, adding hastily, "If you don't mind sharing something so personal."

"If Dr. Adam Vanderleyden had taken over, yes." Doc sighed. "Should've been advertising for another man to take over here soon as I heard about the youngster getting himself killed. But it all slipped by me."

"I see."

Nathan understood a great deal, and guilt stung him. Once again, he had let down the man who had encouraged him to be a doctor, who had been his friend, confidant, and teacher. When he graduated from medical school ten years ago, he should have taken up practice with Doc, as the aging physician had wanted him to. If he had, Doc wouldn't be in this pickle, would probably not be drinking so much, and Nathan might not have lost his sight. . . .

He shut the door on that line of thinking.

"It's clear the woman can't practice in her condition," Nathan said. "I'll see if Corinne and I can talk her out of staying here. Surely she has family she can go back to. Then, when someone else buys your practice, you can pay her the money. Write a letter of intent, and have it signed by witnesses. It will weaken her case if she takes you to court. Besides, by the time her case gets to court, she'll be too far along for any jury to think she should be practicing."

"Thanks, son." Doc sniffed. "That bullet may have taken your sight, but it didn't take your brain."

"No, it missed my brain by a hair." It had simply passed through his head, severing both optic nerves.

Nathan smiled, then turned toward the door.

Doc needed to be left alone now. No man wanted another

man to witness him weeping. Even if that other man couldn't see the tears, he could hear the snuffles and barely suppressed gulps to hold in sobs. Nathan thought perhaps it was the drink weeping, but something nagged at his mind, telling him Doc wasn't that much under the influence.

His hands held out in front of him, he found the opening and made his way across the waiting room.

"Stop!" Corinne cried. "Not another step, Nathan."

Nathan grimaced. He knew he was at least a yard from the top step, since he had just reached the threshold of the front door, but Corinne worried he would hurt himself.

He accidentally pressed his aching left hand against his side and winced. The pain reminded him that his sister worried with good cause.

But he would still finish that carving.

"I gotcha, Dr. Nathan." James, the Maxwell coachman and farm manager, mounted the steps and offered Nathan his arm. "I 'spect you can get down yourself, but we don't want Miz Corinne havin' that baby too early due to frettin' over you."

"No, we don't." Nathan laughed and allowed himself to be guided down the steps and into the landaulet.

The carriage was blessedly open. He sat in the backward-facing seat and curled his right hand over the side for balance.

"Since it's only two blocks to the hotel," he said, "perhaps we could drive around town for a few minutes so I can talk to you, Dr. Vanderleyden."

"Thank you, but there's no need." Her tone was flat, as though someone had drained it of all substance. "I'll get some rest, then contact an attorney."

"Doc doesn't have the money to pay you back," Nathan explained.

James snapped the reins and sent the horses walking forward. The wheels rumbled over the brick street, making dialogue difficult. Nathan wished Corinne and he could take Audrey into the hotel for a glass of lemonade, but she sounded so fatigued, he thought she was indeed better off sleeping right now.

First diagnosing, now prescribing. Old habits die hard.

"He's had a difficult time since his wife died," Corinne added.

"Then he can turn the practice over to me." Audrey sighed. "Those are his choices."

"He can sell it to someone else and pay you back the money," Nathan pointed out. "If you're willing to—"

"No." A jounce of the carriage suggested to him that she'd sat up quickly. Life had crept back into her voice. "I will not go away."

"But surely your family . . ." Corinne began, then her voice trailed off politely.

"My family and my husband's family would be happy to have me back." Audrey's intonation implied a "but."

He waited.

"Then why not—" Corinne began.

Nathan touched his foot against what he hoped was his sister's. Since she stopped talking, he presumed he had nudged the right toes.

"But I would have to agree not to practice medicine—ever. And I promised my husband on his deathbed that I would practice medicine no matter what." Dr. Vanderleyden gave her explanation in a breathless rush.

Was she embarrassed? Ashamed? Lying? Nathan frowned. "I thought he died in a boating accident."

"He didn't drown." Audrey's clothes rustled as the carriage halted. "It was on the Hudson in April. The water was very cold. By the time he was rescued, hypothermia had taken over, and he was . . . too far gone for us to help him. He regained consciousness long enough for—long enough to . . . to obtain my promise. Thank you for the transport."

Before Nathan could scramble to his feet and give her a

hand, she climbed down from the landaulet. Her heels clicked across the walk to the wooden steps of the hotel.

"Was she crying?" he asked Corinne, as their carriage pulled away from the hotel and headed out of town.

"Not yet, but she was about to." Corinne sniffled. "Poor lady. I don't know why any husband would have her make that kind of a promise. Of course, he wouldn't have known she was . . . delicate."

Although he understood Corinne's use of the word *delicate* to mean Audrey was expecting, Nathan couldn't help thinking that she hadn't quite felt delicate in his arms. She was of average height, and her arms were slender but sturdy. Her waist was small above the flare of her hips, save for the telltale thickening in the front. She was far enough along for her husband to have known or suspected her condition. If he'd guessed their families would be opposed to her practicing medicine, he might have extracted the promise as a way to help her keep going despite the pressures against her working.

That is, if the man had extracted such a promise and she wasn't making that up in order to have an excuse to go her own way against everyone's will, propriety, and social convention. She either loved being a doctor or was very good at it, or both.

Doc had been that way once. So had Nathan. Now Doc's heart had gone out of his work, and Nathan's days of doctoring were gone forever, replaced by far too much drink where Doc was concerned and far too little of importance in Nathan's life, including his old friend. Lost in his own tragedy, he'd paid little attention to what was happening to Doc.

"You've grown quiet," Corinne said.

"I'm thinking." Nathan drummed his fingers on the armrest. "You know, Doc isn't a stupid man. Until his wife died, he wasn't a careless man either."

"True. But—Ooph."

The landaulet bounced over the railroad tracks.

"This cannot be good for Russell Junior," Corinne grumbled. "I must stop coming into town, especially since I'm starting to look so unsightly."

"Women in your condition are beautiful, Corinne."

He'd never been able to convince more than a handful of his patients of that, to not lace their corsets in an effort to hide their condition as long as possible, to not give up exercise.

"That's what Russell says, but I feel like one of our pigs just before the autumn."

Nathan laughed. "Corinne, you're absurd."

"And we're diverging from the matter at hand."

"So we are." Nathan tilted his face toward the cool breeze blowing beneath the canopy of trees now lining the road. "You know Dr. Vanderleyden is none of our concern. We're strangers to her."

Corinne sighed. "I know, but goodness, she's alone in the world if she doesn't go back to her family."

"But that's exactly what she must do. Go back to her family." Nathan straightened his shoulders. "If she doesn't, she'll fight to get that practice under her control."

"But I saw that contract," Corinne protested. "I've seen enough of Russell's contracts to know that that one looked legitimate. Even if Doc can't find his copy, surely hers will stand up in court, especially if she can produce the lawyer who wrote up the purchase agreement."

"I doubt Doc's lost his copy." Nathan's hand throbbed around the stitches. "He's not that far gone."

"Then why would he say—" Corinne caught her breath. "I see. He hoped she'd go away."

"Many women would, yes."

"But Mrs. Vanderleyden isn't most women. Still, Nathan, why would Doc do it?"

"Because, as bad as things have gotten for him, the practice is all Doc has left, and if Dr. Vanderleyden takes it away from him, legally or not, think what will happen to Doc."

"I'd rather not."

But Nathan did, as the carriage slowed and trundled up the gravel drive, past fields smelling of freshly cut hay. By the time James pulled the vehicle up beneath the spreading branches of the towering black walnut trees that flanked the farmhouse, Nathan knew what he had to do.

"We need to persuade Dr. Vanderleyden to give up her claim to the practice," he announced.

"Are you against women doctors too?" Corinne asked.

"No, not at all, but—" He leaped to the ground, landing with more of a jolt than he intended, and raised his good hand to his sister to assist her. "I didn't realize how bad he'd gotten until today. He was nervous stitching me, Corinne, and that's not the Doc who showed me that being a good surgeon is a type of artistry."

"He's old." Corinne took Nathan's hand and climbed to the ground.

James pulled the landaulet toward the carriage house.

"He's desperately unhappy," Nathan said. "I think that's why he sold the practice. But I think he changed his mind after he learned the other Dr. Vanderleyden died and no one contacted him for months. He was perfectly sober when I went in there today. He didn't drink until Dr. Vanderleyden walked in waving that contract."

"So you think he's cut back on his drinking?" Corinne squeezed Nathan's hand.

"I think he has. But neither of us has been in town much in the past few months, so we haven't seen him." Nathan turned toward the house with its wide and shady front porch. "We— I've neglected him at a time when he needed friends the most."

Corinne started to lead Nathan up the flagstone walk to the

front steps. "It sounds as though he's done well on his own or with the help of someone else."

"Except look at how he reacted to Dr. Vanderleyden's appearance and claim." Nathan paused with one foot on the bottom step. "He grew distraught, to say the least."

"I know. I grew distraught to see him crumble after being so competent with your poor hand. But, Nathan, what can we do about it?"

Nathan set his mouth in a hard line. "We can do whatever we must to make Dr. Vanderleyden go away."

Chapter Three

In the cool dimness of the hotel dining room, Audrey forced herself to eat. Her stomach tried to rebel with each bite of the delicious roast beef sandwich and blackberries and every sip of the chilled lemonade, but she willed her body to hold on to the nutrition so her head would clear and her baby would grow healthy and strong. She ate every bite because she had paid for the food and couldn't afford to throw away money, unless she planned to return to Connecticut and the loving arms of her family.

A little too loving. They meant well and wanted the best for her. She didn't doubt that for a moment. They simply did not understand her desire to carry on with the profession for which she'd trained and to keep her promise to Adam.

"You're a far better doctor than I am," Adam had said to her, so often it became a tradition at the end of a hard day at the New York Infirmary for Women and Children. "Don't let anyone tell you otherwise."

After the boating accident that sent him floating in the frigid Hudson River for over an hour, when he lay more unconscious than awake, he repeated the litany, adding, "Promise me you will let nothing stand in your way of practicing medicine."

She promised because she wanted an excuse to continue to practice medicine despite her condition.

She never guessed that an aging and apparently grieving Dr. Hornsby would breach the contract simply because one party died. Now she would have to eat into her and Adam's savings, already depleted by the practice purchase, to hire a lawyer. Without income, she estimated she could last a month or less, depending on the lawyer's fees. If the negotiations over the contract took longer than that, she would have to return home.

Home to a luxurious cage, once they learned about the baby.

Finishing the last berry, Audrey rose and headed for the clerk at the front desk. A slim young man with wavy blond hair, he rose the instant she approached the desk.

"How may I help you, ma'am?"

"Can you give me the names of any local attorneys?" She gave him a stiff smile. "Anyone in town, I mean."

"We have two." He grinned. "You know the old saying, one lawyer in a town will starve. Two will get rich."

Audrey laughed. "Let's hope they don't get too rich at my expense."

"No, ma'am. Neither of these men are too rich from lawyering. They're gentlemen farmers mostly. Not enough business around here." The clerk dipped a steel pen into an ink well and then wrote on a sheet of paper. "There's Mr. Tom Buress on Church Street and Mr. Dan Tolliver on Main."

"Which . . . No, I won't ask you to recommend one. That would likely be bad for business here. But if you were to need an attorney, to which one would you go?"

"The hotel uses Mr. Tolliver," the clerk said. "But if I were a lady, I'd go to Mr. Buress."

The clerk answered so hastily, Audrey pressed for more information. "Why?"

"His daughter is studying law in Washington City."

"The world is changing indeed."

Audrey had never met a female lawyer. The law had been slower to admit females to the profession than had medicine, mainly, she figured, because lawyers couldn't study their profession in another country, as she had been privileged to do. Even that had taken considerable effort to persuade her family to let her do, until marriage to a man who encouraged her love of medicine and took her to Paris to study with him had allowed her to realize her ambition.

"Thank you so much for the information." Audrey gave the clerk her warmest smile, making him blush, and left the hotel in pursuit of Mr. Buress.

The town showed a bit more activity now than it had when she disembarked from the train. Several heavy wagons trundled down the street a block from the hotel, and numerous pedestrians meandered from shops and businesses, ladies' pale summer gowns fluttering in a light breeze, the gentlemen tipping their broad-brimmed hats to the females and one another. Not until she stood on the pavement in front of the lawyer's office did she realize that the afternoon had progressed to early evening. The doors along Main and Church Streets were closing. Mr. Buress had already departed. His office was dark, the door locked.

Feet dragging, she returned to the hotel and the steps. She was thankful her room was on the second floor, so she only needed to climb one flight. Two flights might have done her in. Even the fourteen steps to the second floor felt like climbing a mountain. Gripping the polished oak of the banister for support, she climbed to her room.

Without the ceiling fans of the public rooms, her chamber felt like an oven. But the room faced east, and the tiniest of breezes puffed through the open window, bringing the scent of honeysuckle from a vine clinging to a nearby fence and masking the stench of horse droppings from the street. Grateful for the solitude, she removed her jacket, skirt, and blouse and lay on the bed in her petticoat.

No corset. Her mother always said that would get a lady into trouble. Audrey simply never guessed what kind. She didn't think her condition showed enough for the lack of the dangerous confinement of her middle to matter.

It didn't show; Dr. Maxwell had felt the telltale bulge, combined that with her faintness, and reached the right conclusion. Twenty weeks along by her best guess. She had intended to wait until she was quite certain before telling Adam, but when he lay struggling for every breath, she'd told him.

"They'll try to stop you from practicing," had been his gasping response. "Don't let them."

She didn't know if "they" included only their parents or potential patients too. Surely only the former. According to Dr. Hornsby, his patients all wanted another doctor or two in the vicinity, someone on whom they could rely.

She was reliable. She moved her hands to her lower abdomen, wondering for how long she would be.

"I should go home and wait until after the baby comes, Adam." She spoke aloud to the late husband who had been her best friend since they were children. "I can fight this contract breach from home, comfort, security. . . ."

The comforting thought of returning to Connecticut called her to sleep. Then, *Prison,* in Adam's gentle tenor voice, jerked her awake.

She shot upright. The room spun around her, dizzying, disorienting. After a few moments, she realized why. Pale sunlight had flooded the chamber, and a stronger, cooler wind was blowing into the room.

She'd slept all evening and into the morning. And she was

starving. The odors of frying bacon and brewing coffee blew in on the air, and her stomach growled. *Growled! It didn't rebel.* Surely this meant today would prove positive.

After washing and dressing, and bundling her long, dark hair into a coil on the back of her head, Audrey descended to the hotel dining room for breakfast. With the price of the meals there, she decided to look for a cheaper place to eat. For this morning, however, she enjoyed not having her stomach revolt at the mere smell of sausage and eggs and ate well.

By the time she finished, the town appeared to be waking up. Men dressed for business, who had eaten in the hotel dining room also, gathered up hats and strode from the hotel. Following in their wake, Audrey saw shops opening and smelled coffee from the drugstore and an inn down the way. A glance into the windows showed people eating breakfast at both places. She would investigate their prices later.

Finally, her circuit of downtown complete, she approached Tom Buress' office. A sign on his door said he would return in two days' time.

Tapping her forefinger against her lower lip, she stared at her reflection in the window of the lawyer's office and wondered if she should seek out Dan Tolliver, the other attorney. Two days wasn't a long time, but it was time wasted.

Slowly, she traversed the street, passing two banks and a post office. She reached Tolliver's office in time to see Dr. William Hornsby slipping through the door, taking the decision from her hands. She had no choice but to wait for Buress or travel into Winchester. That would take far too long, so she might as well wait.

On the morning of her third full day in Marysville, she presented herself at the office of Tom Buress and breathed a sigh of relief when she found it open. A middle-aged gentleman with silver wings of hair over his temples was just unlocking the door.

"Mr. Buress?" She offered him a tentative smile.

"Dr. Vanderleyden, I presume?" He smiled back. "Don't look so surprised. Your fame precedes you."

"Infamy, perhaps?" She stepped over the threshold into a cool, dim chamber with a glossy pine floor and bright, oriental carpets. "You were gone before I arrived at your office the other evening."

"But word of you arrived at my office long before then. I've already written to my daughter. Do sit down." He indicated a chair upholstered in the same rich red that accented the blues and golds in the rugs.

Audrey sat. She folded her gloved hands in her lap, twisted her fingers together, separated her hands, and rested them on the arms of the chair. All the while, Buress watched her, one eyebrow raised.

"Yes, I'm nervous," she admitted. "I've only gone to lawyers for the contract with my husband and Dr. Hornsby, and . . . and to learn of my husband's will."

"We don't bite if you're the client." He drew out the tall-backed chair behind the desk and perched on the edge, his hands folded on the clean desktop. "So how can I help you?"

"I need Dr. Hornsby to fulfill the terms of the contract." She produced the document from her handbag. "But perhaps you should tell me what your fees are first."

"Let me see what I need to do before we discuss fees." He picked up the contract and began to read . . . and read . . . and read.

He drummed his fingers on the desk while he read. The rhythmic tapping blended with the clop of hooves in the street and click of heels on the sidewalk. A dragonfly zipped in through the open window and began to circle Buress' head, its iridescent wings glowing in a shaft of sunlight.

Audrey pulled her gloves off, then smoothed them back on. She counted the greenbacks in her purse and squinted at her reflection in a tiny hand mirror. She waited . . . and waited . . . and waited.

When Buress set the contract on the desk with a rustle of paper and cleared his throat, she jumped.

"I apologize for startling you, Dr. Vanderleyden." He gave her a warm smile. "You've been quite patient with me."

"It was just so quiet here."

"Marysville is a quiet place, but it's growing. We lost a lot during the war, but in the past twenty-five years, it's returned to a summer haven from the heat and humidity of the Tidewater. We need a good doctor here, and that's no longer Dr. Hornsby, sad to say."

"He doesn't just want to retire?" Audrey probed for more information on the unhappy old man.

Buress sighed. "He made some mistakes after his wife died. Nothing too serious, but enough people stopped trusting him to make him lose his confidence. Nathan Maxwell might have helped him, but he had his own troubles. I think that contributed to Doc's . . . indulgence in spirits when he should be working."

"So people no longer go to him," Audrey concluded.

"Only in desperation." Buress nodded. "But Winchester and Purcellville are too far away really. We were looking forward to a new doctor here."

"So why won't Dr. Hornsby simply fulfill the contract?" Audrey swallowed. "Does he no longer have to because my husband died?"

"If his will leaves you his half of the practice, then, yes, you have the stronger legal footing."

"But?"

"If we can't talk Doc into giving in, you won't have a judge's ear on it for weeks. Not in August around here. Everyone takes a holiday, it seems."

"Weeks." She tried to keep her features composed. "I don't understand. If he's given up, why won't he give in to the inevitable?"

"An excellent question. If you can find that out, you will save considerable fees on my part."

"Then I'd better work that out. I'm not terribly plump in the pocket."

"Begging your pardon for being so vulgar, madam, but even as a Vanderleyden?"

"Yes." She began to tug on her gloved fingertips again. "My husband had a generous allowance. He spent much of it helping me get through medical school, too, and buying the practice. His parents were not pleased with the match when I chose to go to medical school, so they discontinued the allowance upon my husband's death."

They would certainly reinstate it to support her with their grandchild, though. If she gave up the practice of medicine.

"My own parents discontinued my allowance when I got married, naturally."

"So you have limited funds on which to live," Buress said.

Audrey inclined her head in assent and to mask her heating cheeks beneath the half veil of her hat. "And I'm expecting an interesting event by late December."

"I see." Buress cleared his throat. "So time is not on your side."

"No."

In that moment, she wanted to return to the hotel, pack her bags, and hop onto the next eastbound train. Her mother and Adam's would take good care of her. She would lack for nothing except the realization of her need to be a doctor and of her promise to Adam.

She rose. "I'll go talk to Doc again. Perhaps the shock has worn off, and he'll be more sensible. How much do I owe you?"

"Just a dollar to retain me. We'll work out the other fees when and if necessary."

She paid him the dollar. They shook hands, and she stepped into the blazing sun of mid-morning.

She should go straight to Doc's office and try to talk sense into him. Instead, she turned in the opposite direction, heading for the hotel and its dim rooms cooled with electric ceiling fans. Halfway down the block, she stopped, her gaze lighting upon a landaulet drawn up to the curb.

Nathan Maxwell stood beside it, engaged in conversation with—

"Mother?" The appellation burst from Audrey like a cry of distress.

Mrs. Robert Sinclair faced Audrey, her delicate features relaxing into a brilliant smile. "My dear, we were just discussing you with Dr. Maxwell."

We? Even as Audrey wondered at the plural pronoun, Nathan turned toward her with a slight bow of greeting and revealed that Adam's tiny china doll of a mother stood on the other side of him.

"Mother Vanderleyden." Audrey almost dropped a curtsy. Except for her slight stature, Mrs. Vanderleyden didn't resemble Queen Victoria, but her bearing and the way she inclined her head when one talked to her, as though she were looking down her patrician nose at one, gave the impression of royalty, and Audrey felt as though obeisance was expected of her.

"You are looking well, under the circumstances," Mrs. Vanderleyden responded. "You really should have—"

"Good afternoon, Dr. Maxwell." Audrey spoke over her mother-in-law's admonition. "How is your hand?"

"Good, thank you." He drew the injured hand from a chambray glove.

Other than a slight pinkness around the wound, the cut appeared clean, free of infection, and healing well.

"Those are some of the finest stitches I've ever seen." Audrey made no attempt to mask her admiration.

At least she was certain it was admiration for the fine surgery that sent a thrill racing through her as she touched one finger to Nathan Maxwell's strong yet elegant hand.

"Doc used to be a renowned surgeon before the war." Nathan's cheeks looked as warm as Audrey's felt. "After the work he did during the conflict, he came here to set up practice where people really needed him."

"That's what we wished to do." Audrey tightened the corners of her mouth to keep her chin from quivering. "What I still wish to do."

"But you cannot," Mrs. Vanderleyden said. "Not when you're—"

"Later, Iris," Mrs. Sinclair murmured. "We would like to go inside. Out of this sun, Audrey."

"Of course." Audrey glanced at the front door and caught the desk clerk and bellman staring. "Do you have rooms?"

"We do," her mother said. "And Dr. Maxwell gave us a lift from the train. Well, his driver did."

Audrey stared at Nathan. "How did you know they were coming when I didn't know?"

"My, er, sister . . ." His voice trailed off, and his color heightened even further.

"Mrs. Chapman sent us a telegram," Mrs. Sinclair explained. "She was concerned about you."

"Why? She scarcely knows me." Audrey addressed Nathan. She thought perhaps he wouldn't realize she spoke to him, since he couldn't see her looking right at him, but he yanked on his glove and turned to the landaulet.

"That, Dr. Vanderleyden," he said, "you may take up with my sister. But please remember that she is kindness itself. Good day, ladies." With grace that suggested he kept himself in trim physical condition, he sauntered into the carriage.

The driver clucked to the horses, and the equipage pulled away.

Audrey faced the two mothers, her brows drawn together in a scowl. "What are the two of you doing here? And why did Mrs. Chapman contact you?"

"Not out here," her mother said.

"I would like some tea," Mrs. Vanderleyden added.

"And I want an explanation." Audrey headed for the hotel door. "When I left Connecticut, I thought we all understood you were washing your hands of me."

"That was before we knew." Mrs. Vanderleyden didn't say what they knew, as they walked past the clerk and bellman, and Audrey figured it could be anything from Dr. Hornsby's refusal to turn over the practice to . . .

What else would bring the future grandmothers speeding to her by train?

"We'll go in here," she said through stiff lips.

"But your room is more private," Mrs. Vanderleyden pointed out.

"It's also hotter." Audrey smiled at the clerk. "Is the parlor free, Freddie?"

"Yes, ma'am, I'm quite sure it is." He led the way to a door next to the foot of the steps. He knocked, opened the portal, then stepped back so she could cross the threshold onto a fine oriental carpet. "I will bring you some refreshments, ladies." He withdrew and closed the door without a sound.

"Such a fine young man," Mrs. Sinclair said. "I wouldn't expect anyone so civilized out here."

"Mother, we are only a hundred miles from Washington City." Audrey tiptoed across the red-and-gold-patterned carpet, skirts swishing with each stride. "People are quite civilized here."

"Dr. Maxwell certainly is." Mrs. Vanderleyden perched on the edge of a horsehair sofa and folded her black-gloved hands in her lap. "The poor man."

"Yes, it's quite sad." Audrey settled into a straight-backed chair near the window, where a light breeze added its efforts at cooling the air to those of the whirling ceiling fan. A vase of roses masked any unpleasant scents from the street.

"Medicine has lost too many doctors of late."

"And it's going to miss another one." Mrs. Sinclair stood, her spine as straight as the door panel behind her and her chin set as though she were about to lecture a room full of recalcitrant schoolboys.

Or one recalcitrant daughter.

"You will not, under any circumstances, pursue this notion of practicing medicine," Mrs. Sinclair declared, "now that you are carrying Adam's child."

"Who—? Corinne Chapman told you?" Audrey balled her hands into fists against her smooth muslin skirts. "She had no right to interfere."

What was more important now was why she had interfered.

"But we are grateful that she did," Mrs. Vanderleyden said. "Now we can stop you from trying to take that nice Dr. Hornsby's practice from him."

"Take?" Audrey's heart began to pound so hard, she could scarcely breathe. "We bought it from him."

"Adam bought it from him," her mother said, "since the money was his."

"And I inherited it."

"That may be so," her mother said, clasping her hands in front of her waist. "Perhaps one day the doctor will pay the money back. In the meantime, you are coming home with us."

"I am not." Because she realized that sounded like a spoiled child refusing to go to bed, Audrey added, "Adam wouldn't want me to."

"He would want you to take care of his child," Mrs. Vander- leyden said.

"I will, of course. But I have an obligation, a promise to Adam. . . ." Audrey trailed off. She could detect the implaca- bility of the two mothers. Their silence felt so strong. "I am of age," she finished lamely.

"That does not guarantee you are fit to be the mother of our grandchild if you insist on practicing medicine," her mother said at last.

"Of course I am."

In truth, she had deliberately given little thought to the lo- gistics of how she would manage.

"We don't think so," Mrs. Vanderleyden put in. "And we will ensure that others agree with us."

"Others?" Audrey gaped at her, her heart now sending blood thundering through her ears with such force, hearing became difficult. Her stomach turned, and bitter bile filled her mouth. "What are you saying?"

"It's quite simple and clear, my dear," her mother pro- nounced. "If you pursue your claim to the medical practice here and win, we will ensure that you are not able to raise Adam's child."

Chapter Four

The moment he no longer heard Audrey's footfalls ringing across the wooden steps of the hotel, Nathan felt as though the sunshine were a physical weight bearing down on him. He hadn't bothered to stop Corinne from contacting Audrey's mother and mother-in-law. It seemed like the right decision at the time. Dr. Vanderleyden could return home to people who would care for her and her unborn child, and Doc could return to his old self and successful practice.

With his practice threatened, Doc had been sober for days and handled an emergency with his usual skill—the skill that had been lacking since the death of Doc's wife. It had thrilled Nathan to call on his friend and mentor and find the older man stitching up a child's cut knee. Doc had been telling the boy a story that made him laugh so much, he barely flinched at the bite of the needle through his flesh.

Reminded of needles, Nathan rubbed his own stitches. He needed to get them removed in a few more days. The itch of his wound around the thick black threads assured him the wound was healing nicely. As soon as the stitches were out, he would complete his carving. Flawed as it must be, Corinne would appreciate it as a Christmas gift. That gave him nearly five months to complete the work—in secret. Mustn't let James or his wife, Ruby, catch him carving. They would probably confine him to the house like a miscreant schoolboy.

He doubted he should be compared to a schoolboy, but *lay about* fit him, lounging against the side of the landaulet while Dr. Vanderleyden—what? Talked with, argued with, acquiesced to the wishes of the mothers? Nathan didn't know and remained motionless in the sun because he wanted to find out if she was leaving.

When she was leaving. She couldn't stay. She didn't have the money to set up a rival practice.

The sun's heat seemed to be compressing his chest. He needed shade and refreshment. He could climb the hotel steps. Inside were ceiling fans creating an illusion of coolness with their breeze. Except during the war, which he scarcely remembered, they never ran out of ice. He might see Dr. Vanderleyden.

Slowly, he turned his back on the hotel and climbed into the carriage.

"Ready to go, Dr. Nathan?" James asked.

"I should be." He settled into the forward-facing seat.

As the vehicle rolled away from the hotel, he thought he heard the light patter of footfalls across the wooden porch. He would not, simply would not, lean forward and ask James if that was the female doctor.

He leaned forward. "I should stop and look in on Doc again. Is it too late to turn before the railroad?"

"No, sir, it's not." James headed the team down a side street that would lead them around the block and back onto Main Street. As they reached the thoroughfare, he slowed the landaulet. "There's that lady doctor. Do you want to give her a lift?"

"We should offer." Nathan flexed his fingers over the arm-rest.

"Miz Vanderleyden," James called, "you goin' somewhere we can carry you?"

"Thank you, no." Her voice sounded tight and thick, as though her throat were sore. Or clogged with tears.

Nathan opened his mouth to say something—what, he didn't know—but he could no longer hear her footfalls and feared she had gone inside a building or turned down a side street and he'd be talking to air.

He leaned back against the cushions as though he didn't have a care in the world. The carriage maintained its slow pace until it stopped altogether.

"We're here, sir." The carriage shifted. "Let me help you inside."

"I can make it on my own." Nathan stepped from the landaulet. "You stay with the horses."

Finding the first step was tricky. He moved like an infirm man until his foot struck the riser. After that, climbing the treads and crossing the porch to the door was easy. He stumbled a bit on the threshold but kept his balance and walked into the waiting room by himself.

Smiling with triumph, he stood motionless for a moment, listening, discerning whether or not anyone occupied one of the chairs. Voices filtered from the examining room—Doc's and two women's. Two women with familiar Yankee accents. Doc sounded gruff.

"Well, of course you're right," a voice said loudly enough for Nathan to hear the words and not just the tone. "We never approved of our daughter going to France to study medicine."

"She . . . return . . . wardrobe," was all Nathan caught of the other lady's comment.

He didn't need to hear more. The mothers had descended

on Doc. Judging from the snatches of conversation continuing to float through the panels of the inside door, they weren't asking him to give their daughter the keys to his practice.

"If she weren't expecting," the louder woman—surely Mrs. Sinclair—declared, "we wouldn't protest much, even if we don't approve. But since that's our grandchild . . . Well, you can imagine how we feel about her running off."

". . . so soon," Mrs. Vanderleyden added.

Much the same words they'd spoken to Nathan earlier. Dear Audrey had left without a word less than four months after her husband's death. It was unseemly, as if going to Paris to study medicine with her husband and returning to work in the New York Infirmary for Women and Children were not bad enough to create a minor scandal.

Nathan settled into one of the oversized chairs and waited for the discussion to end. Doc would find a way to rid himself of the ladies. Nathan hoped a patient would ring the bell to let Doc know of a new visit, but, although a number of people strolled past the office on the sidewalk, no one mounted the steps.

Moments later, however, the inside door burst open. Attar of roses filled the waiting room, and silk swished. Nathan surged to his feet, prepared to greet the small group.

"Well, I never." Mrs. Vanderleyden gasped between words. "Offering ladies a drink at this hour."

"Or at all." Mrs. Sinclair's heels drummed on the wooden floor. "If Audrey weren't in a delicate condition, I'd think this town would be better off with a—ah, good day, Dr. Maxwell. I didn't see you there."

"I see you managed to reach Doc's before me." He bowed. "You must be fast walkers, as I was in a carriage."

"You were going in the wrong direction," Mrs. Sinclair said. "We came straight here after speaking with Audrey."

"My son never should have married such a stubborn girl."

Mrs. Vanderleyden sniffed. "I like her high spirits, but that doesn't translate well into a wife, does it?"

Uncertain whether or not the question was rhetorical, Nathan said nothing. He feared his comeback wouldn't suit anyway. These ladies didn't want him pointing out that Corinne was an excellent wife after being a rather wild child.

"When you find a wife, Dr. Maxwell," Mrs. Sinclair said, "make sure she's a sweet, biddable girl."

"Yes, ma'am."

As if Mrs. Sinclair had ever been a sweet, biddable girl or wife. Nathan doubted she had gained her commanding presence in middle age. And Audrey had surely learned about determination from someone.

"We thank you again for your assistance in this matter." Mrs. Vanderleyden touched his hand. "Do give your sister our regards and thanks on this matter."

"Will Dr. Vanderleyden be returning with you?" He needed to know—not that it was any of his business. Well, he supposed it was if she was going to stay and drive Doc back to drinking.

"We will stay a day or two and work on persuading her out of her current course." Mrs. Sinclair tramped to the door. "Come along, Mrs. Vanderleyden. We need a rest."

The ladies departed. In the silence left in their wake, Nathan caught the light clink of glass against glass.

His heart sinking, he headed for the inside door, one hand held slightly before him. "Doc?" He opened the door.

Stifling air smacked him in the face. The fumes of spirits mingled with those of carbolic acid.

He wrinkled his nose. "Doc, you're not drinking, are you?"

"You would be too after a visit from those two." Doc thudded the bottle onto the counter. "Was the only way to get rid of them. As if I need anyone from Connecticut telling me how to run my life."

"They mean well—"

"If they mean so well, they should have raised her better." Doc slurped. "Letting one's daughter go to college leads to nothing but trouble. Look at Tom Buress. He's paupering himself so his daughter—his daughter, mind you—can go to law school. As if lawyers weren't bad enough, we've got to have females entering the profession."

Nathan suppressed a chuckle. "We'll only be in trouble when women are allowed to be judges. Now put that bottle away. They're gone, and I believe they will take Dr. Vander-leyden—"

"Don't mention that name in front of me." Doc sighed. "Tolliver tells me the best I can expect is to pay back the money."

Nathan waited.

"I know that's fair," Doc continued in a tone so weary, he might have been twenty years older. "But business has been poor, and I had to live on something."

"Business is doing better."

Even as he spoke, footfalls echoed on the steps.

"Sounds like you have a patient now."

"Yes, things are better." A drawer squeaked open. "If I keep seeing as many patients as I've been seeing this week, I expect I can pay her back in another three or four years."

"Doc, I'll loan you the money if you promise to stop drinking." Nathan hadn't known he would make the offer until the words were out of his mouth.

The ring of the bell in the waiting room was the only sound in the practice for a full minute.

Then Doc moved with a rustle of fabric and a quiet groan as though his joints ached. "I can't take your money, lad. Even if I thought you could afford it, I couldn't make any such promises."

"If you don't, you'll be in debt and without income." Harsh words, but Nathan needed to make up for lost time with his mentor—time he'd spent managing his own grief—if he needed an excuse. "Now, at least, you are rebuilding your reputation."

"For now." Doc headed toward Nathan and the door. "But the loneliness will take over again. One night, I won't be able to bear the silence in the house, and that bottle will start looking like a friend. Or I'll go to the tavern for company and . . . You know how it is."

Nathan sure understood the loneliness. Who was to say that he wouldn't be in the same predicament without James and Ruby watching over him, and Corinne playing mother hen whenever she had the time?

"Can you find companionship another way?" Nathan racked his brains for a suggestion. "Like a wife?"

Doc emitted a harsh bark of mirth. "Only a desperate woman would want a widower like me. My prospects just aren't that good, lad."

"If she kept you on the straight and narrow—"

"Let me know when you find me a desperate woman." Doc elbowed Nathan's ribs. "Now step aside so I can see to my patient."

Nathan remained where he stood in front of the door. "My offer still stands if you want to make a deal. Perhaps the money in hand will send Dr. Vanderleyden on her way sooner rather than later."

"Having those women threaten to take her baby away from her should change her mind faster than money," Doc said.

"They . . . what?" Nathan felt as though someone had kicked him in the middle. "That's coercion."

"Isn't bribing me to quit drinking in exchange for money about the same?" Doc countered.

"This is for your own good."

"And they think their offer is for the baby's own good." Doc rattled the doorknob. "Now run along and find yourself a wife for companionship."

Nathan snorted. "Like you said, only a desperate woman would want me."

The mothers left after two days. Audrey stood on the station platform waving her black-bordered handkerchief until the train curved to the northeast and drew out of sight behind a hill. Then she stuffed the handkerchief into her pocketbook and headed back to town.

"Didn't go with 'em, eh?" the telegrapher called from the station.

"My future is here." Audrey lifted one hand in lieu of goodbye and kept moving.

The telegrapher responded with something she didn't catch, which was probably good.

To herself, she murmured, "At least I hope it is."

Leaving tempted her. Her mother and mother-in-law would drown her in luxury. She wouldn't have to lift a finger for anything unless she wanted to.

That was the difficulty. She wanted to lift her fingers. She ached to hold a lancet, a scalpel, a cone for anesthesia ether. She didn't pine for the gore of surgery but did for the healing results. And then came childbirth. How her arms ached to hold a newborn infant as it took its first breaths. . . .

She paused to wipe mist from her eyes before she fell over something. In four months or so, she would hold her own infant. If she stayed in Marysville and the mothers had their way, she wouldn't hold him or her for long.

Too easily they could have their way. They possessed the money for lawyers to have her child removed from her care. Most people would agree with them. Although happy to have a woman see to specifically female needs like childbirth, even most females didn't want a woman seeing to other medical matters. Women had been midwives for centuries. At least in America, they had only been doctors for decades. Few women would support her right to practice and be a mother without a living husband, she suspected.

If she returned to Connecticut, the mothers would have easier access to her baby. They would keep him if she wanted to return to medicine. Audrey couldn't imagine giving Adam's child up to anyone, not even his grandmothers' care.

If setting up a practice close to her parents and Adam's were possible, she could solve two problems at once. But one reason she and Adam chose the Shenandoah was its dearth of properly trained doctors and midwives. They'd presumed such a condition would make the local people eager for qualified physicians, whatever their gender.

"We were so wrong." She dabbed at her eyes again.

At least about the doctor part. But perhaps people would accept the midwifery part of her profession.

Her eyes cleared. Her footfalls grew lighter, quicker. She reached the hotel and fairly bounded up the steps.

"Dr. Vanderleyden." Freddie greeted her with his boyish grin. "You look well, if I may say so."

"Thank you." Audrey folded her hands at her waist. "Freddie, would you be able to tell me where Corinne Chapman lives?"

"Yes, ma'am." He slipped behind his desk and took out pen and paper. "You'll need a conveyance. It's about four miles from here."

If she went in the morning before the heat struck, she could walk four miles and save money.

"If you take Main Street past the railroad . . ." With a few deft strokes he drew a map. "It's a big house. Almost new. Lots of fancy trimmings on it."

Curiosity radiated from his blue eyes as he handed her the map and instructions.

Audrey thanked him, folded the paper into her pocketbook, and headed out to find some lunch.

She'd taken to buying fruit, cheese, and bread from the

farmers who came into town to sell their wares. That sufficed for an inexpensive lunch. Breakfast she took at the pharmacy, and supper she still ate at the hotel. Thus far, she'd been unable to find anywhere else to stay. The rooming houses were filled or didn't want a single female.

If she earned a little money delivering babies, she should be able to eke out an existence until September, when the judge would return from his holiday.

Walking out to the Chapman estate early the next morning, Audrey decided that if she lost her claim to the practice, she would return home.

The decision left her feeling queasy, and she paused to rest on a rock outcropping big enough to substitute for a throne. Someone had planted phlox around it. They grew up the pale limestone in cascades of pale pink and white, contrasting with Audrey's blacks. In a fit of rebellion, she plucked a few blossoms and tucked them into the high neck of her gown. They held no smell, but the flowers were soft against her chin, and she imagined the way they surely brightened up her unrelieved black.

"I'm already scandalous. What's a little more color?" Laughing at herself, she rose and continued down the winding country road to the second hump of the S curve.

Like arms embracing the tree-lined lane, smooth, green lawns spread around the curve of the road. A pale brown house with scrolled white trim on eaves, window frames, and across the porch roof presided over the vista atop a hill. Black walnut trees flanked the building like sentries, and pastures unfolded beyond.

Audrey swallowed a lump in her throat. If Adam had lived, they would have built a similar house, a place to raise children, a place to discuss patients with each other, a place to grow old.

Despite being married for four years, they had never lived

in a house. Flats had been their way of life. Houses were for someday, a day that would never come.

She'd soon be living in her parents' hundred-year-old mansion or, worse, the Vanderleydens' even older monstrosity if she remained on the road staring at the house instead of calling on the occupants.

She pushed her feet into motion and reached the front door as it sprang open and three children spilled out in a mass of flying limbs and pealing laughter.

"Be careful you don't—Mrs. Vanderleyden." Corinne Chapman filled the doorway behind her offspring. "What are you doing here? I mean, come in. Boys, do not go near the sheep, and stay off the road." She stepped back. "Did you already take your carriage to the stable?"

"I walked." After a glimpse of the elegant foyer with its mirrored tables and vases of flowers, some remaining intact despite the lively children, Audrey realized she should have spent the money on a buggy at least. Thinking these were simple country folk because they lived nearly a hundred miles from Washington City had been a mistake.

"I need the exercise." Her explanation sounded as lame to her as it must to Corinne.

If it did, however, the older woman gave no sign of it. She simply smiled and waved one hand toward a sitting room. "Do come in and sit down. I'll send for some refreshments. Lemonade and gingerbread? It's only midmorning, but you must be starving after that walk."

"I . . . Well . . ." Audrey caught the aroma of freshly baked gingerbread, and her mouth watered. "Thank you. I'd eat gingerbread even if I weren't hungry."

"Good girl." Chuckling, Corinne led the way to the sitting room and pulled on an embroidered rope in one corner. "Someday, I understand that I'll be able to pick up one of those telephones and call the kitchen. Imagine the amount of time and running about that will save."

"Imagine enough telephones so a body can call a doctor to come instead of having to send someone to fetch her." Audrey smiled at her own use of *her* instead of *him*.

Corinne gave her a narrow-eyed glance. "Still determined, aren't you?"

"And you seem determined to stop me, aren't you?"

"Touché."

A maid in black dress and white apron appeared in the doorway. Corinne gave her instructions, then seated herself on a settee. "Make yourself comfortable. If we are going to discuss my interference in your life, I would rather you not be towering over me."

"I won't discuss that." Audrey perched on the edge of a chair so spindle-legged, it had to be at least a hundred and fifty years old. "What's done is done. They'd have found out sooner or later anyway, so no sense in raking you over the coals."

"Thank you. It's too hot for coals. But why did you come?"

"To ask . . ." The words nearly choked her. "To ask for your help."

"I do my best to hinder your endeavors to take over Doc's practice, and you come to me for help?" Corinne's delicate brows drew into a solid line. "I can't imagine why."

"Because—" Audrey stopped, reassessing how she would ask. "First, will you tell me why you telegrammed my mother? Surely you don't care so much about my condition as to think I need a keeper."

"No, it has little to do with you other than the need to get you away." Corinne glanced out the front window.

Beyond the panes and blue velvet drapes, the three boys played baseball with more enthusiasm and shouts than skill.

Corinne smiled at the sight and returned her gaze to Audrey. "I did it for Doc. He was a teacher, a mentor for my brother.

And your arrival had the delightful effect of making him care about his practice again, though he'd do better if he weren't drinking quite so much. That is the not-so-delightful aspect of your arrival—increasing his alcohol intake. But he has already managed to see several patients successfully."

"Then . . ." Audrey thought fast. "With your help, I can assist him further."

"Now isn't that a switch." Sarcasm tinged Corinne's voice. "What can you possibly do to help Doc?"

"Do you think he would be amenable . . ." Audrey lowered her gaze to Corinne's expanding middle. ". . . to my taking the maternity patients?"

"You'd settle for being a midwife?" Corinne shook her head. "I find that difficult to believe. If that's all you wanted, you didn't need to go to medical school."

"More doctors than midwives deliver babies these days." Audrey took on her lecturing tone. "Yet women are so uncomfortable about men handling their most intimate regions that doctors have to examine them and deliver the babies beneath a sheet so they can see nothing."

"Well, of course." Corinne's cheeks grew pink. "But they can use forceps, and midwives cannot."

"I could, or perform a caesarian."

"A what?"

"Never mind that." Audrey smiled. "I have more skills than a mere midwife without medical training. And if you told Doc you'd like me to attend you, he might endorse my work in the county."

"So you can stay and fight your claim to his practice?" Corinne shook her head. "You'll have to convince him yourself. I'll do nothing to see our old friend slide completely into the gutter."

"But—"

"Here is our refreshment." Corinne nodded to the doorway.

The maid entered, carrying an ornate silver tray. She set it on the table beside her mistress and withdrew in silence.

"No, this silver was not buried in the yard so Yankee soldiers wouldn't steal it." Corinne poured lemonade into two crystal glasses from a pitcher with condensation clouding the shimmering surface. "My husband's father was a blockade runner and made an indecent fortune. No old money like the Vanderleydens and Sinclairs. What a heritage your child will have."

"Only if it's a boy." Audrey rose to accept her glass and plate. "We girls just get married off."

"So they'd find you another husband if you went back?" Corinne raised her glass as though toasting with the pale yellow liquid.

Audrey nodded. "I'd be pressured into it with the reminder that I am a pauper in my own right."

"So things aren't all that different up north." Corinne sighed. "I do wish I didn't like you, Mrs. Vanderleyden, but I do, so I'll offer you a compromise."

Audrey held her breath, glass poised against her lips. The sweet tartness of the lemonade tickled her nostrils and made her thirsty. But she waited.

"Make your offer to Doc. If he goes along with you, I will too."

Chapter Five

Dr. Hornsby would never accept her proposal without Corinne Chapman's support. Going to his office was a waste of time, but time was one commodity Audrey could afford to waste at present. If a miracle occurred and he went along with her idea, nothing would be lost and much would be gained.

So Audrey told the Chapmans' coachman to set her down in front of the surgery instead of at the hotel as Corinne had instructed him to do. To Audrey's relief, he didn't argue with her but simply stared at her with pale green eyes.

He would tell his mistress about the change in direction. Not that Audrey cared. If Corinne wasn't going to sponsor her, Audrey had little to lose except her freedom and the opportunity to practice any form of medicine.

She grimaced at her sarcasm and mounted the steps.

Two people sat in the waiting room, a man with a swollen and bandaged foot, and a bilious-looking woman of indeterminate years. Resigned to a wait, Audrey settled in one of the chairs and took out her fan. Besides stirring the air, it was a good shield against conversation.

The two patients kept casting surreptitious glances her way, and she feared they would start talking. If they did, she feared she would start diagnosing and prescribing.

None of them spoke. The street outside fell silent without passing vehicles or pedestrians, and voices flowed through the inside door, loud enough to identify the speaker, not loud enough to hear the words. Nathan's voice was calm, smooth, and rich like warm custard. How soothing he must have been to anxious patients.

How soothing the tones were to her.

She found herself straining to catch the words for a moment, then returned to fanning, as if trying to shove the voice from the room. No widow of less than four months should endeavor to hear the voice of another man because she liked it. In truth, she should leave before that man departed from the surgery.

She remained seated, waiting.

Moments later, his hand wrapped in a fresh bandage, Nathan exited the examining room. A shaft of sunlight from the open door fell on his face, drawing golden lights from his hair and turning his eyes the rich blue of a summer sky.

Audrey's stomach plummeted down her middle. She felt breathless and weak-kneed like a schoolgirl with her first tendre—one Audrey had never felt about Adam, her best friend.

She shot to her feet, ready to bolt.

"What do you want?" Doc shoved past Nathan and glared at her.

"To make you an offer." Audrey inclined her head, hiding her face with the brim of her hat. "After you see your patients, of course."

"I'll keep Dr. Vanderleyden company." Nathan spoke with haste, as though trying to prevent Doc from saying something. "You see to these other people."

The two patients stared in openmouthed silence.

"Come in, Mrs. Neff." Doc held the door wider.

The yellowish lady rose and stalked past him with the stiff-limbed movements of an automaton. The door closed behind her, and her voice, nearly as deep as a man's, reverberated through the panels. "It's my liver again, and that doctor in Winchester will do nothing about it but tell me to stop drinking."

"Funny she'd come to Doc about that." The man with the bandaged foot guffawed. "If this gout didn't make me so uncomfortable traveling, I wouldn't be here."

"You need to stop drinking your homemade wine, Jasper." Nathan took slow steps down one side of the room, then the other.

Audrey jumped up, fought dizziness for a moment, and touched his arm. "May I help you to a seat, Doctor?"

"Thank you." A tide of red washed up from his high white shirt collar. "Beside you, maybe?"

"Certainly." Audrey took his hand and led him to one of the wide chairs.

He wore no gloves, and the warmth of his skin radiated through her lace mitt, heating her more than did the summer day. She tried to let go the instant he stood before the seat, but his fingers clung for a moment, applying unnecessary pressure.

With an effort, she resisted the urge to squeeze back. As handsome and charming as he might be, he was the enemy—sort of. At least he fought against her effort to get control of the practice. She admired him for that loyalty to his friend. She also disliked him for that loyalty.

The gouty gentleman Nathan had called Jasper frowned. "Why'd you let yourself get shot like that, Nathan? We need a good doctor here."

"You have a good doctor here." Nathan settled in the chair. "If we can keep Doc from drinking—"

Jasper snorted. "With the anniversary of his wife's death coming up? Not likely."

"Is it?" Nathan rubbed his bandaged hand. "I don't know when it happened precisely."

"You were too busy being merciful and getting shot," Jasper grumbled.

Audrey glanced at Nathan, wanting to ask what had happened but knowing it was rude.

"So my sister says you've decided to stay, Dr. Vanderleyden." Nathan changed the subject with blatant abruptness.

"She's a doctor?" Jasper asked.

"I am." Audrey felt her chin jut as she waited for his retort.

"Do you know what I can do for gout?" Jasper looked as eager as a puppy awaiting a treat.

Audrey laughed. "My free advice is no red wine and no roast beef."

"And what would you recommend if I paid?"

"No red wine and no roast beef," Nathan and Audrey said together.

They laughed.

Jasper scowled and, with the aid of a walking stick, pushed himself to his feet. "I may as well save my dollar if that's all Doc will do." He stomped from the surgery, cane thumping, bandaged foot dragging. "Give up my pleasures. Humph," he muttered until his voice died away in the rumble of wagon wheels on the street.

Silence reigned in the waiting room. The bilious lady's voice rumbled on in complaint. Though gruff, Doc's responses sounded surprisingly gentle and understanding.

A twinge of nausea plucked at Audrey's stomach. For the second time, she witnessed Doc's ability as a physician.

"His wife was everything to him." Nathan broke the stillness in a voice so low, it registered barely above whisper level. "They lost their son in the war. Their daughter married an

Englishman and has never returned to America. Their son was a doctor, so when I expressed interest in the profession, Doc took me under his tutelage. I owe my success to him."

"And I owe my failure to him." And her husband for insisting on sailing on the river in early April.

The nausea increased, and she wrapped her arms across her belly, feeling the thickening at her waist as a reminder of another cause for her current dilemma.

"I've thought of a compromise," she blurted out. "What if I took over the female medical needs of the county, and we formed a partnership?"

"You'd settle for being a midwife?" Nathan arched brows that were so perfectly shaped, they looked plucked.

"It's a foot in the door."

Even before those perfect brows drew together in a frown, Audrey knew she'd said the wrong thing. She knew Doc would never accept her offer. He would view even the simplest of midwife duties as her way of trying to wedge him out and prove to the county she was a better doctor.

"Well, why did he sell the practice if he wants to keep working?" she asked with some frustration.

"He needed the money." Nathan rubbed his forehead, smoothing out the frown and mussing the waves along his hairline until they stood up like a pompadour.

Audrey clasped her hands together to stop herself from smoothing down his hair.

"But he needs the work more. Since you came here and reminded him how important the profession is, he's done better than he has since his wife's death." Nathan sighed. "If I could be of use . . . Dr. Vanderleyden, go home. We'll all be better off without you in the long run, and you are in no physical condition to be traveling around a mountainous county at all hours of the day and night."

"But—" She snapped her teeth together, counted to ten, and

rose. "Perhaps you're right." Without bidding Nathan good-bye, she left the office.

She began to walk. She passed the hotel and railroad tracks, a field of cows, and a stand of towering oaks. Her feet carried her along the shady lane leading to Corinne's house.

Her thoughts carried her farther, back to Union Station in Washington onto a train headed for New York and another one, for Connecticut. Away from the rural valley where she and Adam had planned to settle, raise their family, and practice their profession. She envisioned a future with her medical diploma tucked away in an attic for her children to find and wonder about while she presided over charity teas.

Her entire being rebelled. She pressed her hand to her mouth to stop herself from crying out, "No, no, no."

She wanted a home and a family. Since Adam's death, she experienced a sense of emptiness every day, as though a vital organ had been removed. He'd been her best friend if not the Prince Charming of every schoolgirl's dreams. Knowledge of the baby helped. Knowing she could still take over the country practice kept her going.

Two weeks earlier, traveling to Marysville and taking over the practice seemed like the best of ideas. The confines of mourning stifled her after a lifetime of constant activity, and the mothers smothered her with their well-meaning kindness. The practice meant freedom.

Now, however, even without the mothers' threat to take her child from her and Dr. Hornsby's resistance to her claim of ownership of the practice, Audrey began to doubt the rightness of her actions.

Legal right to the practice or not, she could not take it over if it meant sending Dr. Hornsby back into the depths of despair. At the same time, she'd made a promise to Adam. Keeping her word to him to practice medicine, no matter what, was the least she could do after failing to love him as much as he had loved her.

She would have to find another place to practice—somehow.

Not having an answer for that dilemma and too weary to think, Audrey headed back to town. When she was halfway there, a farmer pulled up his wagon and offered her a ride.

"It's too hot to be walking, ma'am." He handed her a basket brimming with glistening blackberries. "Don't have anything you can drink, but a handful or two of these oughta help."

"Thank you." Audrey popped a succulent berry into her mouth.

The sweetness burst on her tongue, and she nearly purred.

"I'll take the whole basket." She spoke without thinking of the price. "I mean, how much do you charge for them?"

His ruddy face creased in a grin. "Nothin', ma'am. They grow wild along the sides of the road, and it keeps my young'uns out of trouble pickin' 'em. Just bring the basket back when you're done." He gave her directions to his farm.

"If I forget," Audrey said with a mouth full of berries and forgetting her manners, "I'm at the hotel."

"I know you are." The farmer drew up at the end of Main Street. "You're the lady doctor."

"Yes, I am. If I can ever be of assistance . . ." She trailed off, realizing she probably wouldn't be in town long enough to assist anyone. "I'll do what I can to thank you for your kindness." She climbed down from the wagon and headed toward the hotel with as much speed as she could manage without appearing to flee.

Several businessmen stood around the front desk with their luggage. What they came to the small town to do, Audrey couldn't imagine. She appreciated their presence, for she managed to slip by Freddie unnoticed and reach her room without speaking to anyone. With the door locked behind her, she set the basket of blackberries on the dressing table and collapsed onto the bed.

She needed to sleep more. Fatigue was part of her condition and a reason both men and women gave for ladies not being supposed to work in her delicate condition.

Delicate indeed. She was strong and healthy, just a bit tired. And no wonder. She had walked over ten miles in the past two days. Yet she couldn't sleep. Heat, noise from vehicles and trains, the stench of horse leavings from the street, and her own writhing thoughts kept her from napping during the day and from sleeping at night.

After two days, she knew what she had to do, as onerous as it was and bleak though it made her future. A waste of all her years of studying and struggling.

Trying not to weep even behind her veil, she made her way to the train station to purchase a ticket for the following day. No matter if it took most of her remaining funds; she would no longer need to worry about money once she reached Connecticut. Besides, she would still pursue the matter of the money owed her by Dr. Hornsby.

Her skirts feeling as heavy as armor, and the telegrapher's smirk burned into her mind's eye, she dragged herself up the steps of the hotel. Not until she entered the lobby, and the breeze from the whirring fans swept across her sticky cheeks, did she realize how oppressive the air outside had become. The gauze veil of her hat disguised the diminished sunlight. Good. Perhaps a storm would clear the air and cool things down.

Part of her wanted to remain in the lobby and enjoy the relative coolness. The other, sensible part of her reminded her she needed to pack.

She obeyed the sensible part and trudged toward the stairs.

"Dr. Vanderleyden," the clerk called, "you have a caller."

"Please give whoever it is my regrets." She kept up her pace to the stairs and up.

"But, Doctor." Freddie sounded a bit frantic.

Audrey quickened her pace, ignoring the footfalls pattering behind her.

"Doctor."

She closed and locked her door as thunder rumbled in the distance.

She went to the window to search for the flashes of lightning. Now, her hat removed, she saw the purple-black clouds rolling from the top of Mount Weather like a lid sliding over a box. Forks of silver-blue light split the clouds, and thunder rolled in their wake, echoing and re-echoing from the Blue Ridge to the Allegheny Mountains. *Boom. Boom. B—*

She jumped. That wasn't thunder. Someone was pounding on her door.

Go away, she thought.

Her medical training warned her to answer the summons.

"Coming," she called.

At the same time Freddie shouted, "Dr. Vanderleyden, please. It's an emergency."

An emergency?

Audrey charged the two remaining yards to the door, shot the bolt back, and flung the portal wide open.

Freddie stood in the corridor, his face greenish white, one hand clamped to the elbow of Nathan Maxwell. Nathan's color was also paler than normal, and his right hand clutched his left. That hand, now without its white bandage, dripped blood onto the carpet.

"Got to see to Mrs. Chapman." Freddie gulped. "She fainted in the lobby."

And he bolted toward the stairs.

"What happened?" Audrey asked. "Never mind. Come in." She grasped Nathan's abandoned elbow and ushered him into her chamber, where she turned him so his back was to the bed. "Sit."

"Yes, ma'am." He sat. His eyes widened, and he stood again. "This is your bed."

"There's nowhere else to sit, and you look like you're about to fall."

She pressed her hand to his shoulder, urging him down. With her other hand she yanked the case off of the pillow and pressed it against the bleeding hand. "Hold this in place. I'll be back."

Despite the cost, she was glad of the bathroom. It gave her swift access to water. After a moment or two, it ran clear and cold, and she soaked one of the towels in the flow.

"Now tell me what happened so I know what I'm dealing with here." She carried the dripping towel into the bedroom.

"Doc." Nathan closed his eyes, fanning his gold-tipped lashes across the top of his broad cheekbones. "He slipped while removing the stitches."

"Slipped." Audrey kept her tone neutral as she removed the pillowcase and pressed the cold, wet compress to the wound. "For someone who made those beautiful stitches, I find that difficult to understand."

"No, you don't." Nathan opened his eyes and looked at her so directly, she thought he could see her. From no more than a foot away, the blue of his eyes proved achingly intense. "You're already thinking he was probably inebriated."

His voice held an accusation, as though the doctor's drunkenness were her fault.

"I thought you wouldn't let a man in that condition remove stitches." Audrey took away the cold compress.

The bleeding had slowed. She now saw the new gash amidst a network of severed black threads.

"Hold this here while I fetch my things." She took his free hand and held it over the wet towel and injured palm. "I'm going to have to pull out these stitches and sew it up again."

"Do you . . . I mean, can you . . ." He was white at the lips. "I mean, do you have the equipment?"

"Of course." Audrey's lips twitched.

Good thing he couldn't see her in this case. Not fair to laugh because the doctor was such a nervous patient.

She hastened to pull her medical bag out from under the bed. "I have a small bottle of carbolic, so I can disinfect the needle and thread. It's been boiled once and kept in a silk bag since, but one can't be too cautious." While she threaded a needle and splashed carbolic acid over her hands, needle, and thread, she talked about what she was doing and her philosophy of cleanliness. "Keeping bacteria away from the wound site is the most important part of healing. More surgical patients and women die from post-procedure infectious fevers than from the wound or birth itself." She wetted a strip of cotton waste with carbolic and touched it to the wound.

He sucked his breath in through his teeth and growled something deep in his throat.

"Why, Dr. Maxwell," she purred with exaggerated sweetness, "I do believe that was unrepeatable."

"And not half of what I was thinking." He managed a smile so sweet, she stuck the needle in a fraction farther than she intended.

He repeated the unrepeatable as she fixed her gaze on his hand. Nothing should ever distract the surgeon from her work. Not even an attractive man.

Kneeling on the floorboards before him, she completed her work with as much speed and as little discomfort to the patient as possible. The resultant row of stitches pleased her. They were even tinier than Doc's had been, thanks to all her years creating embroidery samplers as a child.

"Give me one moment to bandage that." She caught hold of his right hand. "Don't touch it. You haven't washed that hand."

"Instinct to look." His color returning, he smiled up at her.

Audrey was glad she still rested on her knees. She doubted she could have remained upright in that moment.

Good thing she was going home the next day. This attraction was madness, betrayal of Adam's belief in her, disloyalty to his love for her. If she couldn't grieve him as much as she should, she should at least give him a year of mourning.

But Nathan had laced his fingers with hers, and she didn't want to move.

A knock on the door sent her rocketing to her feet. "Who . . . who is it?" She sounded guilty.

The door sprang open. Freddie, Corinne Chapman, and two elderly matrons visiting town clustered around the doorway. From the narrowed eyes and pinched lips of the ladies and Freddie's smirk, Audrey feared she looked guilty too.

"Leave us." Corinne sailed into the room. "I see you've put my brother back together."

"Yes. Yes, he'll be just fine." Audrey licked her dry lips. "It looks like a lot, but he didn't lose that much blood. He still may wish to . . ."

Nathan squeezed her hand, and she realized she was babbling.

"Rest," she concluded.

"I'm glad you were able to manage that debacle so easily." Corinne sighed, looking in need of rest herself. "Now we need to work on the other problem this has caused."

"Other problem?" Nathan glanced toward his sister, brows raised. "Something to do with Doc, I'm afraid?"

"I'm afraid not." Corinne's gaze dropped to her brother's hand, the one still holding Audrey's. "The reason may be of the purest intent, but you know how gossip travels in this county, and too many people know you've been alone in a hotel room with this lady for the past thirty minutes."

Chapter Six

Nathan glared at his sister. From the sniffs and clearing of throats, he knew she wasn't alone, so he held his tongue rather than tell her what he thought of the implication of her words.

Audrey proved not to be quite so restrained. Her indrawn breath warned him she intended to speak. Still holding her hand, he squeezed her fingers in an attempt to stop her.

"I am attending an injured man." The purr of Audrey's voice dropped to a soft growl. "Your precious Dr. Hornsby made a mess of the stitches removal, and I have spent all of these thirty minutes tending to it." She grabbed his wounded hand and held it up like a display in a medical course. "Or did you think I could do this work in five minutes and spend—" She stopped on an exhalation of air like an engine letting off excess steam.

Nathan resisted the urge to draw her hand to his lips and kiss the smooth back.

"She was stopping me from losing the use of my hand too," he said instead.

Someone caught her breath.

"She is a doctor," Nathan concluded.

"Which is why females shouldn't be physicians." The female voice was unfamiliar but the tone of censure, common. "No lady would ever be alone with a man to whom she is not married."

"Doctors are alone with patients of either s—gender all the time." Audrey sounded more composed, though her fingers held his in a vise grip. "Others aren't always available to provide a chaperone, as in this situation."

"Then it's not a respectable profession for a woman." It was a different female voice this time.

"Corinne." Nathan stood, fighting the nausea he'd experienced since Doc slipped with the razor-sharp scissors. "You know what happened. Why are you here with these people and making such a fuss about the only help I could get on short notice?"

"You're still holding her hand." Corinne coughed in the artificial way people do when covering up a laugh. "What else was I supposed to do but remind you to behave yourself?"

"Of course we were behaving ourselves." The growl returned to Audrey's voice. "I am a doctor."

"You won't ever doctor my husband," one of the women declared. "I don't know how you can bear to have her turning one of your rooms into a surgery, Freddie. Who will ever want to sleep on that bed again?"

"Well, um—" Freddie cleared his throat. "The parlor was occupied, and I didn't think the dining room would work. But I thought I'd return in five minutes to . . . er . . . supervise."

"You were going to supervise?" Nathan didn't bother to mask his laugh. "Freddie, you would hardly add to Dr. Vanderleyden's consequence if you'd been in here too."

"If I hadn't fainted . . ." Corinne heaved a gusty sigh. "Oh, la, how the rumors will spread. My brother will be ruined."

"Scarcely likely." Audrey released Nathan's hand, leaving his fingers feeling cold. "I'm leaving tomorrow."

Cold seeped from his fingers into his chest.

"Leaving?" was all he could think to say.

"A good thing," the lady strangers chorused.

No, it wasn't, Nathan wanted to respond.

Yet he had spent the past two weeks working toward this very outcome. He should be happy about her decision. It was best for all. Doc's ramblings, which should have warned Nathan that the old man had been drinking though he didn't smell of alcohol, indicated he was feeling maudlin because of his wife's being gone and other wives not knowing their place. Nathan knew the old man meant Audrey and hadn't taken the bait. Nathan wanted Doc concentrated on removing the stitches and not on the lady threatening to exert her rights to his practice.

Doc had been doing so well. Nathan wanted to be able to show everyone the healed hand and be able to say his mentor was on the mend.

Nathan wanted to be able to say that the county could trust Doc again. Then Doc could restore his patients, pay Audrey back so she could leave, and let matters continue with everyone, if not happier, at least more content.

Now she was leaving with nothing resolved, and Nathan felt anything but contentment coursing through him.

"Why?" Nathan asked.

"It's apparent to me," one of the harpies said. "No one wants her here."

"Maybe the city likes female doctors," the other stranger put in, "but not this place. Freddie, it's a good thing she'll be removing herself before she ruins the reputation of the hotel."

"Doc's good when he's sober." Freddie inserted his opinion.

"But he isn't these days, is he?" Audrey must have been clenching her teeth. "He slipped because he was inebriated. Dr. Maxwell could have lost the use of his hand. But you think Dr. Hornsby better than I am because he's a male and I'm a female?"

"He has a lot more experience." Corinne drew closer to the bed, her footfalls light for a lady so heavy in her condition, her lilac perfume floating above the lingering sharpness of carbolic.

"And he's dangerous," Audrey muttered.

"I should have known better than to go to him today." Nathan reached out his good hand, hoping to find, with success, a bedpost for support. "I knew the anniversary was coming up, but I didn't have anyone to take me into Winchester."

"A doctor can't afford to have a day so bad he injures a patient." Audrey's tone held a lecturing note, a hint of hauteur and superiority.

Nathan leaned his shoulder against the tall bedpost and gave her what he hoped was a cool glance, something to distance them. "What happens if your labor pains come upon you suddenly, while you're performing a delicate procedure?"

The ladies in the hallway gasped and muttered about disgraceful talk.

Audrey dropped onto the mattress with a rustle of skirts and creak of ropes. "Your hand should heal nicely, Dr. Maxwell. Seek medical assistance if you experience more than normal tenderness, swelling, or discharge." Cool professionalism radiated from her. "Now, if everyone will excuse me, I would like my room to myself so that I may pack."

"Dr. Vanderleyden, I—" Nathan reached out his hand to her. He touched a coil of soft hair before the bed creaked again, and he no longer sensed her close or smelled her blend of carbolic and lilies of the valley.

"Let's leave her for now." Corinne took his arm. "Freddie, you will send up a maid to clean up this mess, won't you?"

"Yes, but there's blood on the coverlet." Freddie gulped. "I'll get into trouble for bringing Dr. Maxwell up here if that isn't paid for."

"Add it to my bill," Audrey snapped.

"Nonsense." Nathan turned his head toward her. "It goes on mine. And I owe you for your services."

"No, you don't." Her voice gentled. "It's professional courtesy not to charge another doctor."

"But I'm not a doctor now." A silence followed his words, lasting too long for anyone's comfort, least of all his.

Then her skirts rustled. Her spring-flower scent filled his nostrils like a heady vapor, and she touched his cheek. "You're a doctor, Nathan Maxwell. More than that, you're a true friend to William Hornsby. If you stay by him, he'll be successful in overcoming his weakness and becoming a doctor everyone can depend on again."

"And what will you do?" After wanting her to go elsewhere for his friend's sake, now he wished for her to stay a moment longer.

"I'll go somewhere away from here to be a doctor. I cannot practice medicine in this town knowing I've possibly driven a man into despair."

Words failed Nathan. Once, he'd thought he was smooth-tongued and charming to the ladies. Now he felt as tongue-tied as an adolescent with his first crush.

Except that with Audrey Vanderleyden he was not an adolescent, and mere puppy love did not begin to describe the feelings crowding his chest.

"Thank you." He squeezed out the response and headed for the door.

Never had his sister's need to guide him humiliated him more. Nonetheless, he kept his head high, exiting the room as the nosy matrons scattered like the hens they were. The door clicked shut behind them, the lock snapping into place.

"I thought I was doing the right thing." Freddie rushed past them but must have been walking backward from the direction of his voice. "I couldn't have her performing surgery or whatever she had to do in the public rooms. But I should have sent up one of the maids. The problem was, I couldn't have them going all squeamish and fainting. And I was worried about you, Mrs. Chapman. I do like Dr. Vanderleyden, but it's a good thing she's leaving."

"I think so." Corinne's fingers tightened on Nathan's arm.

He said nothing on the way down the steps and into the sultry air left behind by the brief storm. He said nothing until they reached the waiting carriage. Settled on the backward-facing seat, he glowered at his sister across from him.

"What was that scene for?"

"For the sake of the biddies gossiping in the parlor about you being in a female's room. I wanted them to see for themselves that you were being doctored. But, truly, Nathan, why were you holding her hand like that?"

"Because I couldn't gaze into her eyes." He managed a smile. "I believe she did an excellent job. The pain is less."

At least the pain in his hand was. As for the pain in his heart . . .

"I thought it would help if she was stitching you up or something when we walked in." Corinne sighed. "I was thinking of your reputation more than hers. We can't have people saying you are a womanizer if you want to marry one day."

Nathan snorted, thinking of what Doc and he had said. "Only a desperate woman would want me."

"Oh, Nathan, don't be such a goose. You are a fine-looking man, and you have an excellent property and income. You're intelligent and . . . But we've discussed all this before. I'll never convince you."

"No. But you can tell me why you thought you could salvage my reputation at the cost of Dr. Vanderleyden's."

"I thought we wanted to be rid of her, especially after Doc's relapse today."

"Yes, of course we do." Nathan cradled his injured hand in his good one. "I really thought he was all right. I was so proud of him. Encouraging him made me feel . . . useful."

"Then keep working at it. It's been too short a time for a big difference straightaway. You as a physician should know that. In the meantime"— she laughed—"come home with me, and I'll show you how useful you can be letting the children climb on you instead of me."

"They have Russell for that."

"Not tonight. He's overseeing a shipment of something from Alexandria." Corinne gave a sniff too exaggerated to be real. "He used to take me with him but won't in this condition."

"So you really want my company." Nathan smiled at her. "Thank you, but Ruby promised me a chicken pie for dinner, and that won't keep another day."

But Ruby didn't have the pie made. When Nathan entered the house, it echoed with silence, and no delicious aromas of baking chicken and pastry wafted from the kitchen.

"Ruby?"

No response. No slap of the carpet slippers she preferred to shoes.

Feeling as though his modest farmhouse had become an echoing mansion, Nathan wandered from room to room. If she'd fallen while sweeping or dusting, she could be anywhere. He might walk right past her or trip over her and make matters worse.

Reaching the back door, he realized he should have called for James straightaway. He would have the horses put up by now and might be wondering about his wife's whereabouts himself.

Nathan opened the door. Now, if he could make his way to the stable without losing direction . . .

"Dr. Nathan?" James' voice went high on the name. "Dr.

Nathan." His footfalls pounded along the gravel path to the house. "You gotta come. It's Ruby. She's done had an apoplexy or something."

Audrey cleaned the room herself. Since she didn't want to go outside her chamber for fear of meeting the disapproving matrons, she took the maid's cleaning things and tidied up after her impromptu surgery.

If only she'd been bandaging Nathan's hand, no one would have questioned her behavior.

It doesn't matter now. She leaned her brow against the window glass cooling in the twilight. *Tomorrow I'll go do what everyone thinks is right—give up medicine for motherhood.*

If only she felt it were right.

Too heavyhearted to eat, she settled down with her lap desk in an attempt to compose the telegram she would send before she boarded the train. "You win," although it was true, made her sound a bit too much like a sulky adolescent.

Dr. Hornsby won, she hoped. She would press her suit to regain the money, but that was all. If he could remain sober long enough to regain his patients' confidence, he would pull through. He would have a purpose in life. That was what so often kept patients alive. Surely it worked for the grieving too. Knowing she had the practice and wouldn't be buried under too much sympathy for long had kept her going after Adam's death.

She shuddered to think how much sympathy and loving care she would now receive in her condition. The imminent arrival of Adam's child, who dared not be anything but a boy, would be treated like the imminent arrival of a royal prince.

She set the lap desk aside and rose from the bed. The dining room closed in a quarter of an hour, and she really shouldn't skip dinner. She also needed to tell Freddie to wake her early enough to catch her train.

Seeing that her hair was a mess, she removed the pins and began to brush out the tangles. It fell in waves around her shoulders, long and thick, rippling from right above her ears to the ends at her waist. She wondered how much of a scandal she would create if she simply braided it and left it hanging down her back. Too much, alas. She couldn't count the times she had held scissors in her hand, tempted to start cutting.

She was beginning to twist it into its usual knot on the back of her neck when a knock sounded on her door.

"Who . . . is it?"

"Freddie, ma'am. There's an urgent message—"

Audrey yanked open the door. "What's wrong? Dr. Maxwell?"

"His housekeeper's taken ill." Freddie eyed her tumbled hair. "The carriage is waiting for you."

"I'd best hurry then." She snatched up a shawl, her doctor bag, and a black grosgrain ribbon. As she hastened through the lobby, hair floating behind her, she caught sight of half a dozen persons in the dining room who stopped eating and talking to stare at her. She flashed them a smile, knowing she was giving them gossip fodder for weeks to come.

Outside, rain had begun to fall again, but James stood beside the carriage, waiting to assist her inside.

"Dr. Vanderleyden, thank you for coming." His dark face crumpled as if he was about to cry.

"My Ruby, she's took bad. Dr. Nathan told me to fetch you. He said you was closer. But I didn't know . . ."

"Of course I'm coming." She exerted a gentle pressure of reassurance on his arm. "Let's drive as fast as we can and still be safe in this rain."

He took her at her word. She didn't think she'd ever raced down a country lane as fast as James pushed the horses. Fortunately, unlike the road on which Corinne Chapman lived, the Maxwell farm was set along a relatively straight thoroughfare. Unfortunately, mud slowed their progress and sent the carriage jouncing so much, Audrey staggered when she alighted.

In the dark, with only James' lantern to guide her, she could see little of the house or surrounding area. She caught the whiff of a stable—more hay and horse than anything else, which indicated good care. James led her up a flight of steps running alongside a building near the stable. She thought perhaps it was a carriage house.

"Dr. Nathan's in there." James opened the door. "I gotta see to the horses. Stable boy's asleep by now. You be all right, ma'am? I feel kinda funny draggin' a lady out like this at night."

"I'm used to it." Audrey smiled at him, then entered the tidy apartment.

Light and the murmur of voices drew Audrey through the sitting room to a bedchamber.

Nathan sat beside a brass bed, a lantern above him turning his hair color to molten bronze. As her heels echoed on the wooden floorboards, he glanced her way.

"Dr. Vanderleyden?" He looked a bit uncertain.

"Yes. I came at once."

She was glad he couldn't see her with her hair streaming down her back, confined by a mere strip of ribbon tied into a lopsided bow.

"And this is Ruby?" Audrey approached the bed on the opposite side from Nathan.

"Ruby Buck," he confirmed. "She and Corinne fight over who will mother me, don't you, Ruby?"

"Yes, sir." Ruby's words emerged on a wheezing breath. "But I win."

"Then we'll be sure you'll win against whatever's going on here." Audrey took the woman's hand, testing her pulse while studying her face.

Ruby was probably in her mid-fifties with graying black hair tightly braided though not pinned up. Her dark complexion held a grayish cast to it, and her eyes were dull. Her pulse was fast but not racing.

"May I?" Audrey drew down the sheet and rested her ear against the older woman's chest.

Her heart sounded a little too loud, pumping a bit too hard, but it was strong and steady.

Her breathing, however, concerned Audrey. Each inhalation and exhalation brought a wheezing rattle with it.

She straightened. "Can you tell me what happened?"

"You tell her . . . Dr. Nathan." Ruby closed her eyes, gasping.

"She said she was picking dandelion greens right before the storm." Nathan's face grew pensive. "She said she was having a hard time catching her breath, so came back here and lay down. She doesn't remember much after that until James returned."

"Hmm." Audrey studied Ruby's face as she listened to her wheeze. "Mrs. Buck, did you pick anything besides dandelions? Or were there other weeds nearby, like goldenrod or ragweed?"

From the corner of her eye, she saw Nathan nod as though approving of her question. Ridiculously, she thought, she felt a tingle of pleasure at the silent praise.

"There always be weeds about." Ruby took several breaths. "And they was mowing the front acres nearby."

"Ah." Audrey glanced at Nathan. "You've already figured this out, haven't you, Doctor?"

"I don't diagnose anymore."

Audrey scowled. "Don't be ridiculous. You can diagnose this as easily as I can. It's asthma."

"It's what?" Alarm rang in Ruby's voice, and she tried to sit up. "Am I gonna die?"

"Easy. No." Audrey pressed a hand to her shoulder, holding her down. "We don't know exactly why, but sometimes some people just can't be around things like weeds and fresh grass, or even cats, dogs, and horses. When they are, they start to wheeze like you. Sometimes it gets so bad, they can't catch their breath and think they're having a heart seizure."

"It isn't my heart?" Ruby appeared to calm a bit. "But I can't breathe right."

"We'll do what we can for that." Audrey glanced around, wondering where the kitchen was. "We need boiling water, camphor or mint or eucalyptus, and these windows closed."

"There's no kitchen up here," Nathan said. "We'll have to move her to the house."

"Is there a room ready there?" Audrey headed for the door. "Tell me where, and I'll start preparing things."

"There's mint in the garden." Ruby sounded bewildered. "But I can't go stay in the house."

"Of course you can." The tenderness in Nathan's tone squeezed Audrey's heart. "James will carry you there."

Audrey met James coming up the stairs. She gave him instructions and reassurances, started to lead the way to the house, then remembered Nathan. He needed help getting back home.

She returned and offered him her arm. "Where will I find mint?"

"In the garden." He tucked his hand into the crook of her elbow. "There should be camphor somewhere in the kitchen. I-I don't know much about . . . it."

"I think you know a great deal more than you're letting on." Audrey led the way along a gravel path from the carriage house to the main house. Lanterns hung above the doors, guiding her way. James followed, carrying Ruby with the gentleness with which someone carried a newborn and murmuring reassurances to her all the way as she protested.

"They've been married since they were sixteen," Nathan said. "I don't know what they'd do without each other."

"They shouldn't have to if we can get her breathing under

control." Audrey hesitated on the threshold. "Is there a woman close by we can have stay here? After the debacle this afternoon, I'd prefer we have a chaperone if I'm going to stay."

"I'll send James for Sally Bishop. She's the wife of one of the farmhands and lives nearby. It'll give James something to do besides worry."

Once Ruby was settled in one of the bedrooms, James headed off to fetch Mrs. Bishop, and Audrey set about building a fire in the hearth so she could keep steam in the room. It would become unbearably hot, but the heat and steam redolent of camphor would ease Ruby's breathing. She doubted she could find the mint in the dark, but she found some dried chamomile in the kitchen and made tea.

Nathan sat at the table in a little breakfast room, drinking the cup of tea Audrey poured for him and saying little. She wished she had something for him to do but didn't know what. She would have had him fetch and carry, but he couldn't read the labels on the jars. If she knew of some tactile way he could read . . .

She started. "When I was in Paris, I heard of a Frenchman who made up a way blind people could read. Have you ever read—heard about this?"

"I have." Nathan looked pensive. "Braille. Louis Braille was his name. But not many people know how to teach it."

"No, I suppose not. But if someone could . . ."

Again she trailed off. She couldn't learn Braille and teach it to him. She wouldn't be around for that long. And, for now, in the hours remaining to her in the Valley, she needed to help Ruby Buck breathe normally again. Getting the older woman to stop fretting was a first step.

"If you drink your tea and rest," she admonished Ruby for perhaps the tenth time, "you'll be up and about a whole lot faster."

The arrival of Sally and James helped. With the sweetest of

smiles, James ordered Ruby to do whatever the lady doc told her to do.

Sally, tiny and quiet and around Audrey's age, took in the room in a glance and snatched up the bucket. "I'll fetch more water."

She continued to act with efficiency, anticipating Audrey's needs. Near midnight, Ruby's breathing grew less labored. Her restlessness in sleep calmed. Sally and Audrey exchanged warm glances of appreciation for a job well done and leaned back in the armchairs James had carried in for them.

"I can stay if you'd like to lie down, ma'am." Sally yawned.

Audrey laughed. "You're as tired as I am. I can sleep here."

"Then so can I."

Audrey leaned her head into a wing of the chair and closed her eyes. "I'll wake if her breathing changes."

She woke to the crowing of a rooster, a brisk wind shredding the clouds to reveal blue sky, and the knowledge that she had missed her train.

Chapter Seven

For a moment, hearing Audrey give Sally nursing instructions, Nathan experienced a stab of regret so profound, he wasn't sure he could face her. He should be the one giving orders on a patient's care. He should be the one spending the night in the sickroom, ensuring the treatment worked and devising something else if it did not. He should have been the one diagnosing Ruby's condition in the first place.

He had, in truth, suspected the source of her problem. He'd seen her struggle for breath before and wondered if it only happened at certain times of year or when she'd been around animals. He knew she never entered the stables unless absolutely necessary, and she protested against any kind of pet in the house, much to his regret, as he loved dogs and cats.

He needed Ruby, and he had nearly lost her because he dared not diagnose.

Things he did dare to do were shaving himself and starting a fire in the stove. Everyone feared he would slit his own throat or burn down the house. So far, however, he had only nicked himself a few times and managed the stove well enough to ensure the household had hot water for washing and to get a pot of coffee going.

This morning was no exception. By the time he heard foot-falls on the steps, the smell of coffee was beginning to perme-ate the kitchen. Not knowing if Sally or Audrey approached, he ran his hands over his face, inspecting it for missed beard stub-ble. The skin felt smooth save for a scar on his chin from one of his early efforts with the razor, and his hair, always a bit un-ruly, stuck up more than it should. He'd forgotten to comb it. He'd been in such a hurry to impress Audrey with his ability with the stove that he'd neglected basic grooming. What would she think?

He was beginning to wonder why he should care what she thought, when she entered the room and took a deep breath.

"What a wonderful smell. Did James come in yet?"

"No, I expect he's getting the haymaking started." Nathan grinned. "I made coffee."

"That's incredible." She came near him, bringing the scent of camphor with her. "Do you make breakfast too?"

"No, I'm not that talented." He grinned. "I couldn't cook before either."

"I can't cook either. Maybe Sally can take the time to cook for us." She touched his arm. "May I examine your hand?"

He tried to draw away. "It's all right."

She held on tightly to his wrist. "I expect you know what you're talking about, but I'd rather see for myself."

"Wouldn't you prefer coffee first? Or tea? We can put the kettle on for water."

"I had some peppermint tea with Ruby this morning." She cradled his injured hand in hers, her fingers as soft as petals against the back of his hand. "You've gotten the bandage grubby."

"Stoking a woodstove fire is dirty work."

"And infections are unpleasant." She unwrapped the bandage and touched his wound.

He caught his breath.

"Sore?" She traced the wound. "It's a little infected." Her voice changed so that he knew she tilted her face up to his. "Why did you say it was all right?"

Nathan shrugged. "I was going to soak it later. You've enough to concern you, and if you're . . . leaving today, we've imposed on you long enough."

The words choked him.

"I already missed my train."

"I'm sorry."

Except he wasn't, which was nonsense—he'd been instrumental in her decision to leave.

"I never should have called you out here."

Especially not after favoring his friend and mentor over her.

"I'm glad you did. Mrs. Buck needed care." Audrey's fingers flexed around his hand. "Of course, you knew perfectly well what was wrong with her, didn't you?"

He shrugged.

"Dr. Maxwell." She emphasized the professional appellation. "I saw you approve of my diagnosis last night. So why didn't you diagnose and treat?"

"I'm not a doctor anymore. I couldn't be sure—"

"That she couldn't breathe or that it started when she was around the weeds and hay?" She dropped his hand so abruptly, it swung behind him and bumped the worktable.

He gritted his teeth against a stab of pain.

"You also knew your hand was infected." She stalked to the sink, her heels thudding on the pine floorboards. "But you were going to let it go?"

"I misdiagnosed Doc yesterday and caused trouble for you." He ran the forefinger of his right hand over the neat stitches on his left palm. "I thought he was merely sad. I smelled no alcohol. I didn't hear it in his voice."

She started pumping water. "Some alcohols have no scent." The water stopped. "And you haven't caused any trouble for me. I don't care about a little gossip about me in a town that has already made it clear they'd rather have a man who isn't sober most of the time than me for their doctor."

"He's been sober nearly two weeks." Nostrils flaring, Nathan turned to remove the coffee from the stove and close the burner so the brew would stay warm without growing too strong. "If I'd been any kind of a friend or physician, he wouldn't have fallen this far. And Ruby . . . I should have known what was wrong with her a long time ago. She probably shouldn't be out in the country, at least not at this time of year."

"Is moving into town a possibility for her?" She came toward him again, water sloshing against metal. "I'll heat water so you can soak that hand."

"I could send her in to take care of Doc. Maybe if he weren't alone so much, he would take better care of himself."

Something else he should have thought of sooner.

"But then I'd be in a bit of a bind." He gave her a half smile.

"Sally said she's happy to work. She could cook and clean for you."

Nathan gave her a mock ferocious glare. "You're just as managing a female as my sister."

"You'll be rid of me soon enough." She sounded weary.

He reached out his good hand to her but didn't quite know where she stood, so he missed making contact. "How soon can you get another ticket?"

"I expect they'll exchange it." She opened the firebox, sending a blast of heat pouring into the kitchen. "If Mr. Buck can drive me back to town today, I'll take care of that, but. . . ." She dropped wood into the stove. "I'd like to come back out.

Mrs. Buck will be capable of travel in a day or two, and she should have someone with her."

A day or two. He could keep Audrey near for a day or two.

"We can arrange that." He hesitated. "Tongues will wag indeed."

"We'll have Ruby and Sally for chaperones. The gossips can talk all they like. I'm leaving."

"But I have to live here, and if I am not exactly an eligible bachelor, I am a bachelor."

"Not eligible?" She faced him. "Dr. Maxwell, why in the world wouldn't you be eligible?"

"Because—"

James arrived then, saving Nathan from having to point out the obvious to the lady doctor. Also preventing him from continuing to talk to her, for she set Nathan's hand in a bowl of warm water and salt and took James up to see Ruby.

Audrey departed after that. While Ruby slept, Sally cleaned the kitchen and fed the chickens. Eggs gathered, she made Nathan breakfast, then went to sit by the patient.

Nathan retreated to the front porch to sit in the sunshine, which was not so fierce after the rains of the day before, and yearned for a book he could read, two good hands with which to take up his carving again, something to do. He heard the workers mowing the hay, smelled its pungent freshness, and wondered if he could bale. With the birds nearly quiet in August, the farm was too quiet, too isolated from people.

Perhaps he should move into town, where neighbors lived close at hand. He wouldn't have to endure so many long silences then.

Although the chiming clock on the parlor mantel told him no more than three hours passed, the time until Audrey's return dragged. When he heard the carriage wheels rumbling up the drive, he half expected James to tell him that she had decided to stay in town or, worse, catch the afternoon train. But she greeted him from the vehicle.

"Freddie sent out a basket from the hotel kitchen," she called to him. "Something about owing Mrs. Buck a favor?"

"He does. I'd forgotten about that. Their cook got sick one day when they had a number of guests staying in town for a wedding, so Ruby took over the kitchen and saved the day." Nathan rose and descended the porch steps and followed the sound of her voice and the shifting of the horses to the carriage. "Did you bring your things?"

"I did." She rested her hand on his shoulder and stepped to the ground. "I also called on your sister to tell her."

Nathan groaned. "She'll be here later, I have no doubt."

"She will. She's bringing supper." Audrey laughed. "She was more than a little shocked when I admitted I couldn't cook."

"Ha, she can't cook either." He crooked his elbow, hoping she would take it.

In his own home, he could be the one doing the leading.

Instead of taking his arm, though, she tucked the handles of a basket into his hand. "Take that to the kitchen, if you please. I need to see to my patient."

He winced. With a simple action, with a few words, she reminded him she was at the farm for Ruby's sake, not his.

He carried the basket to the kitchen. The aroma of roasted chicken and fresh bread wafted from the contents. He could unpack the food, set out plates, and have the table ready for her when she returned downstairs. If she would eat with him.

She did share his meal. Between visits to her patient she joined him outside, bringing news of doings in town, asking about Ruby's progress, and offering to take him for a walk.

"I need the exercise." She stood in the doorway, smelling of flowers now instead of camphor or carbolic. "And you look bored."

"I am." He held out his arm.

This time, she put nothing into his hand. She tucked her fingers into the crook of his elbow, and they headed down the drive.

"What do you do with yourself all day?" she asked.

"I try to remember medicines and anatomical terms and physiology." He snorted. "I don't know why. It's useless to me now, but I spent so much time learning it, I don't want to forget it."

"I can understand that." She was quiet for several yards. "Will you tell me about your practice? Did you have a special area of interest?"

"Obstetrics." He tilted his face to the light breeze. "My patients were all rich women who expected the best care money could buy, so I volunteered time in the slums too. Too many of the midwives there were dirty or unwell, and women were coming into the hospital so much in extremis, we couldn't help them. So I tried to take as much cleanliness and good practices as I could to them. I like to think I prevented a few deaths."

"Working at the women's infirmary was like that for me." She spoke in a low voice as though fearing she would disturb someone. "I wanted to work at a big hospital, but they weren't willing to have a foreign-trained female around, so we bought the practice down here."

"Why not Connecticut?"

"They have enough doctors. There don't seem to be enough down here."

"No." He paused where his drive met the road. "Right or left?"

"Right. Does it have something to do with the war?"

"Yes. Many doctors were killed, then people didn't have the money to go for training. Then, of course, we didn't have a lot of men left. I was only eight when the war ended."

"That's really tragic." She slowed her pace. "Were you injured while in the slums? Or should I mind my own business and tell you to forget that question?"

"It's all right. Everyone knows."

Everyone knew what had happened. No one knew of the cold knot of fear for his future that tightened around his heart every time he talked about the incident. Yet he wanted Audrey to know that, even if he was of little use now, he had been a hero of sorts. "I was coming home from a lying-in and heard a fight. A man was down, a sailor. I stopped to help him, even though some men told me to stay away. I wasn't going to leave a wounded man bleeding in the gutter. So someone shot me."

"I'm sorry." Her hand squeezed his arm. "What a loss for you and your patients."

The tenderness in her touch and the maple-syrup richness of her voice eased the pain.

"It's why I had to save Doc. If I couldn't practice, at least I could help him regain his." He turned his head toward the cawing of crows in a nearby field. "I'd heard some rumors, but I didn't realize how bad off Doc was. That day you saw me in town was the first time I'd been anywhere but here or at Corinne's since . . . I recovered."

She said nothing. Their footfalls, crunching on the gravel in unison, and the cawing of the crows were the only sounds amidst the meadows, trees, and fields of corn and hay.

He feared he had offended her. Thinking back over what he'd just said, he realized his faux pas even before she drew in her breath and replied, "You don't mind *my* being unable to practice?"

"Dr. Vanderleyden." He stopped and turned toward her, holding her hand in his as though he feared she would run away. "You will get the money back from Doc eventually. You can set up practice elsewhere. You're young and determined enough to succeed anywhere. But please understand that I couldn't—can't—let a friend continue to slide into despair and ruin."

"I do understand. It's why I'm leaving." Her fingers moved inside his clasp, though she didn't try to pull them away. "I will leave as soon as you've made arrangements for Ruby and she's out of danger."

"I wish—"

Unable to tell her what he wished, he started walking again, still holding her hand. He knew the path along the road so well, he scarcely needed anyone to guide him. But he liked the company and having someone to talk to. So he searched for a safer topic of conversation.

Before he could, she took a breath so audible, he expected a lecture.

"What do you miss most?" was all she asked. "Besides practicing medicine, of course."

"Reading." He hadn't realized he had a ready answer until she asked the question. "I used to read for hours. Medical journals from here and from Great Britain. Novels. Anything."

"Would you . . . Would you like for me to read to you?"

In that melodious voice? His heart melted with joy at the suggestion.

"Thank you."

They returned to the farm. After Audrey tended to Ruby, she returned to the front porch and seated herself beside him. The rustle of paper told him she'd brought a book with her.

"I found *Jack the Fisherman* by Elizabeth Stuart Phelps. Have you read it?"

"You want to read me a novel written by a female?" He turned away so she couldn't see him smile.

He felt her glare and disapproval in silence, and he laughed.

"No, I've never read Phelps, but I'm willing to try. She can't be more sentimental than one of the Brontës."

"Very well." She sounded a bit stiff.

Once she began to read, however, her voice flowed like honey warmed by the sun. She could have read the Montgomery Ward catalog and he would have enjoyed it. Time slid past like a silent runner. Shadows grew longer, and shade from the walnut trees slanted across the porch. The rumble of the mower in the hay field ceased, and, moments later, carriage wheels reverberated along the drive.

"That will be Mrs. Chapman." Audrey closed the book. "I'll go look in on Ruby."

Before he could protest or thank her, she dashed into the house, letting the storm door slam shut behind her.

Nathan stood as the carriage drew to a halt. From inside the vehicle, Corinne's voice floated out, directing someone to take a basket into the house. Then the door opened, and she climbed down, breathing a little harder than she should in, his medical opinion.

"Why the frown?" Corinne asked as she mounted the steps.

"I didn't notice I was frowning." He held out his hands to her. "Are you all right?"

"I'm afraid this is going to be one of my last excursions." With a sigh, she sank into the chair Audrey had vacated. "With the other three, I managed to go out until the last two months, but I've grown as big as a pachyderm and want no one to see me this way."

"Twins?" He tucked his hands behind his back.

He wasn't a doctor. He had no right to examine her.

"The midwife says no. Now sit down and tell me why Mrs. Vanderleyden ran off the minute I arrived."

"She was reading to me." Still frowning, he sat. "Are you certain you didn't mistake what date you expect your confinement?"

"As certain as a body can be. But I am not discussing my condition with you. The midwife is perfectly competent."

"And lives fifteen miles away."

"Perfectly adequate. Now, tell me, how do you like having Mrs. Vanderleyden around?"

More than he would admit to his sister.

"She's done well with Ruby."

"And took you for a walk today."

"Walked with me, yes." The turn of the dialogue struck him, and he grimaced. "How did you know about the walk?"

"You passed three farms. I had two callers tell me about it." Corinne's tone became slightly teasing. "I understand you two looked rather cozy."

Nathan shrugged. "Holding on to someone makes the going easier. You know that."

"You don't hold hands with anyone else you walk with."

His cheeks grew warm in the coolness of the shade.

Corinne laughed. "Ah, brother, you have the most open face. And you can't even see how pretty she is."

He set his lips in a firm line in an attempt to close his face.

Corinne simply laughed harder. "So we'll discuss something else, like what you intend to do about Ruby needing to be away from the country."

"Sally can come in and cook and clean." He breathed a silent sigh of relief. "And James can manage the farm."

"And what if you have another accident like cutting your hand open?"

"I can install an alarm bell?"

"Nathan, I'm being serious. I don't think you should be out here all alone at night."

"The idea doesn't appeal to me either, but I don't have much of a choice, except perhaps taking rooms in town."

"If you could find something suitable, which is doubtful."

He narrowed his eyes and turned toward her. "All right, Corinne, when you start objecting to my life and the plans I make for it, I know you have something in mind."

"Oh, yes, dear brother." Corinne sounded smug. "I have something quite special in mind."

Chapter Eight

"I can't leave Dr. Nathan." The fervor of her protest increased Ruby's wheezing. "He can't be here all alone."

"Calm yourself, Mrs. Buck." Audrey rested her hand on the older woman's shoulder. "I understand why you don't want to leave Dr. Maxwell, but your health is suffering out here right now."

"But what'll I do in town?" Tears filled Ruby's dark eyes. "I've worked all my life. James and me saved every penny we could for when we can't work no more, but that'll be a long time yet."

"You'll still be working." Audrey picked up a cloth soaking in a bowl of fresh, cold spring water and wiped Ruby's perspiring brow. "You can take care of Doc. Imagine how happy Dr. Maxwell will be if you're there to see to his old friend and keep him from drinking himself into an early grave. And all while you're away from here, where you're risking your own health."

Ruby drew her brows together. "Are you saying I could die if I stay out here?"

"Yes, I'm saying you can." Audrey wrung out the cloth and repeated the cooling ablutions.

With the windows closed against the fine dust kicked up by the mowing, dust that made Ruby cough uncontrollably, the bedroom was as stifling as a laundry room.

"You came too close to breathing your last yesterday."

"It was just a spell. I'm better now." As if trying to prove it, Ruby struggled to sit up.

Audrey held her down. "You need more rest. Tomorrow will be soon enough to get up."

"But, Dr. Vanderleyden, who's gonna take care of Dr. Nathan?" In her struggle to breathe, Ruby's question sounded petulant.

Audrey swallowed an impatient response. She knew setting a patient's mind to rest was nearly as much a part of the healing as was the treatment. She needed to reassure Ruby that Nathan would have the care and attention he required.

"Sally has agreed to cook and clean."

Even as she spoke the words, Audrey knew they weren't enough.

"Sally lives all the way on the other side of the farm." Ruby gave Audrey a disgusted look. "He can't get help from that far away. Besides that, who will take him for walks? James won't have the time, driving back and forth as he'll have to be doin'."

She, Audrey, would.

Even while holding the cold washcloth, Audrey's hand felt warm from Nathan's touch during their stroll. She'd enjoyed the camaraderie of sauntering along the country lane with rolling cow pastures and woods on either side of them. Honeysuckle, wild roses, and fresh hay had permeated every sense like a banquet. She had savored each breath and wanted to bottle it like perfume to take out and remember. . . .

What was she thinking?

She dropped the cloth into the bowl of water with a splash.

"Perhaps he can go stay with Corinne. This is only until the first frost."

"Humph. Dr. Nathan wouldn't like that. She manages him too much."

"And you worry about him like you're a mother hen and he's one of your chicks." Audrey went to the door. "He's a grown man, Mrs. Buck, and not as helpless as everyone thinks he is."

"Humph." Ruby slapped the bedspread. "He likes my attention."

"Yes, and you've been good to him. But now it's time to let him pay you back a bit." Audrey opened the door, relishing the relatively cool air rushing in from the hallway. "You rest now. I'll bring up your supper in a quarter hour or so."

"You don't do that. Send James up."

"That's a wonderful idea." Audrey slipped out and stood in the cool dimness of the hall for a moment.

Nathan and Corinne's voices drifted up through the open window at the end of the corridor, the words indistinct, the tone serious. Clattering pans in the kitchen indicated that Sally was busy, presumably warming up the dinner Corinne had said she would bring. Despite four people being close at hand, Audrey felt isolated, alone, perhaps more alone and isolated than she had in the hotel.

In the hotel one encountered other people on their own, or knew nothing of their lives and thus had little reason to care about them except as human beings. One knew nothing of their families, their fears, their hopes for the future. Here, Audrey knew how Ruby worried about Nathan and not being able to work, and how she missed her husband. She knew about Corinne's discomfort and frustration with the confinement of her condition, and how Sally didn't want to seem too eager to take over Ruby's work and have extra income for her family. Most of all, she understood Nathan's fear of being useless and having too little to do for the next forty or fifty years of his life.

Yet, in spite of her knowledge, Audrey knew that none of them needed her. When she left, they would think she'd been a bit of an annoyance, useful in bringing Doc's problems to light so he could get help, and able as a doctor to help in a crisis. Other than that, they would be relieved to see her go.

In contrast, the mothers would welcome her with open arms, a stool on which to prop her feet, and endless rounds of nourishing teas, jellies, and broths. She wouldn't have to lift a finger.

She wouldn't get to lift a finger, not during her confinement, not to care for her child, not to support herself and the baby. Once she sat in the clutches of the overly protective mothers, she would never get away unless she gave up motherhood for medicine. She would never fulfill her promise to Adam.

The day before, her decision had seemed right. Surely, Adam would prefer she raise their child to her using her training to heal strangers. Yet now that she had seen two patients, she remembered how much she loved being a doctor, seeing the sick grow well and the injured healed. Now, gazing across the rolling fields of the Shenandoah Valley, she knew she could in no way return to the isolation of the Sinclair or Vanderleyden estates, where she would have everything she needed—including a husband if she asked for one—except for usefulness.

The only difficulty with her decision to stay would be how to survive. If not for the impropriety of their being young and single or for her inability to cook, she would offer her services as Nathan's housekeeper. Perhaps Corinne would need a nanny. With three boys and baby on the way, she might appreciate assistance other than a nursemaid's. She could teach. She could be around and act as companion when Corinne reached her confinement and her condition kept her housebound.

Lighthearted with the solution, Audrey descended the stairs to find out if indeed Corinne had brought dinner and when the food would be ready, and to look for James. The aromas of roast beef and creamed potatoes met Audrey halfway down the steps. She inhaled, and her stomach growled. Smiling, she continued into the kitchen.

"Everything's ready, ma'am," Sally greeted her. "I'll just go out and tell Mrs. Chapman and Dr. Maxwell."

"I'll go." Audrey started toward the front door, then stopped. "Will you fix up a tray for Mr. and Mrs. Buck to have up in the sickroom?"

"Yes, ma'am. Is she up to eating?" Sally began loading plates onto a wide wooden tray.

"She's doing well." Audrey strode through the dining room and parlor to the front door, opened it, and stepped into the fresh breeze sweeping the scent of hay across the front porch. "Dinner is ready. Are you staying, Mrs. Chapman?"

"No, I need to get back to my brood." Corinne made no move to rise. "But I'd like a word with you before I go."

Stomach knotting, Audrey briefly closed her eyes. "A word?"

"Corinne, I forbid you to say a word." Nathan's color was high.

"Did I do something to offend you?" Audrey folded her hands together over the slight bulge of her middle to keep herself from brushing her fingers across his brow and testing for fever.

"On the contrary." Corinne's eyes danced. "Now, if I speak, I'll displease my brother."

"Then, by all means, don't." Audrey turned toward the door. "Dinner is ready, thank you, Mrs. Chapman."

"Go on in, Nathan." Corinne nudged her brother's foot with the toe of her brown leather shoe. "I want to talk to Mrs. Vanderleyden."

"And I'd rather you didn't." Nathan didn't quite speak through his teeth, but a muscle jumped in his jaw.

"Perhaps . . ." Audrey glanced from brother to sister, the former scowling, the latter grinning. "I should be the one to go in."

"You do that. I'll take my brother into a field and abandon him somewhere so he can't interrupt me."

The idea was so outrageous, Audrey laughed. "Perhaps you should let her talk to me, Dr. Maxwell."

"You may be right." With an exaggerated sigh, he stood and headed for the house, his footfalls so unerring, he might have been able to see his way with clarity.

"He's amazing, isn't he?" Corinne cast a loving glance toward the closing door. "Two years ago you'd think he was no better off than a newborn. Now I'm not so sure he'd be lost in the middle of the field if I did drop him off in one. He's got ears like a cat. If only he could do . . . something." Her tone grew wistful.

Audrey perched on the edge of the chair Nathan had vacated. "Not being able to practice one's chosen profession is frustrating. The boredom must drive him a little mad."

"It does. He misses reading, besides the medical practice, and teaching."

"He could still teach, couldn't he? Anatomy or—"

"Don't." Corinne held up her hand. "We've tried to get him to approach medical schools about teaching. But he won't leave his family. With the way trains are now, he would never be that far from us, but he couldn't live on his own."

"Ruby and James?" Audrey glanced upward. "Getting out of the country would be good for Mrs. Buck. I've recommended it."

"Yes, but they've lived here all their lives. I think a city would frighten them. I still hope." Corinne cocked her head to one side. "Maybe you can be a good influence on him."

"I won't be here long enough to be an influence on anyone." The words settled a heaviness around Audrey's heart.

"Yes, so I hear. You're giving up and going home." Corinne frowned as though she disapproved.

Audrey swallowed. "I don't have a choice. My funds are limited, and no one here needs me."

"My brother does."

"I beg your pardon?"

Corinne laughed. "Don't look so shocked. You know you've made yourself indispensable to him these past couple of days."

Audrey stiffened. "Not, I assure you, for any nefarious reasons."

"Of course not." Corinne patted Audrey's arm. "You wouldn't still be talking about leaving if you had. And I don't think it's in your nature."

"Thank you." Audrey didn't relax.

"I wouldn't be asking you this if I thought you were a designing female." Corinne shifted on her chair, pressing one hand to her lower back. "There've been a few of those already, females who think they can take advantage of him because he can't see. He's not wealthy by Vanderleyden standards, but he's comfortably off. He could hire a secretary, someone to read to him and keep him company, but he doesn't think it's fair to keep the sort of person he'd like this far out of town, let alone a city. They'd have to be pretty well educated, you see, and most men with that kind of education are already gainfully employed. The ones who aren't, one wouldn't trust to hire."

"Very true," Audrey murmured.

"And of course a female wouldn't do." Corinne plunged on, talking a little faster. "The impropriety would ruin her."

"Yes." Audrey began to suspect where Corinne was going and braced her legs, ready to spring to her feet and bolt.

"Unless . . ." Corinne met Audrey's gaze and held it. ". . . she was married to him."

Chapter Nine

Nathan reached the small breakfast room off the kitchen, where he usually took his meals, before he admitted to himself he should have stayed on the porch. He should have made Corinne keep her wild notion to herself if doing so was possible.

Audrey Sinclair Vanderleyden didn't want another husband. It wasn't as though she needed a name for her unborn child's good name. Whether male or female, that child possessed a brilliant future. If Audrey bore a boy, he would be heir to the Vanderleyden wealth and privilege and would grow up to be anything he liked, so long as he chose something prominent or prosperous. If the child turned out to be a girl, she would look forward to a life divided between good works and the pursuit of her own pleasures, so long as those pleasures fell within the acceptable boundaries of society.

Unlike her mother.

Audrey had kicked over the traces of societal expectations for a woman, especially one of her background. College was growing more acceptable for females, but entering the professions was another matter. A few women doctors married. Most married other doctors.

Unlike him.

Regret weighing down his heart as much as thoughts of Audrey pressed down upon his mind, Nathan ran his fingertips along the chair rail on the breakfast room wall, finding his way around the chamber. In the kitchen, china clinked and cutlery chimed; liquid splashed, and the aroma of roast beef and creamed potatoes wafted through the warm, summer air. Sally was serving the dinner his sister had brought.

Nathan's stomach clenched but not in hunger. It was more like fear, apprehension, and shame. On the other side of the house, Corinne was making a marriage proposal for him.

All right, not precisely a proposal. She was planting the idea in Audrey's mind.

It was a profoundly bad idea for Audrey. He could think of a dozen reasons why he should marry her. He could think of only one reason why she should marry him—no one could take her child from her then. Whether or not she could still practice medicine as his wife was another matter. His instinct said no. After working so hard to get Doc back on the right path to recovering his reputation and practice, and thus his reason for living, Nathan couldn't see himself allowing Audrey to take over patients who might otherwise go to Doc.

But if they didn't interfere with Doc's patients, if they wouldn't go to him anyway for whatever reason . . .

His heart's desire vying with loyalty to an old friend, Nathan approached the bay window and let the cool breeze fan his hot cheeks. In no way would a woman like Audrey consider marrying a man like him even for the sake of her child. She was too strong, too driven, and probably still too much in love with her husband to think about remarrying, let alone someone as useless as he seemed to be to those around him. All he had to offer her was a home, a good name, and . . . his heart.

"Dr. Nathan?" Sally spoke from behind him. "Do you want your dinner now, sir?"

He didn't, but if he didn't eat, Sally would stay until he did. That would keep her from her own family.

"Yes, you can serve it." He didn't turn around, afraid of what his face might reveal of what his head and heart were telling him. "Will you ask Dr. Vanderleyden if she would like to join me? She's on the front porch with Mrs. Chapman."

"No, she's right here." Audrey's velvet voice slid over his ears like soothing fingers on an aching brow.

Nathan's heart filled his chest and tightened his throat.

"Corinne has gone home," she added.

He smiled. "So it's Corinne now, is it? How did you two get so friendly all of a sudden?"

"Since she decided she was tired of my four-syllable last name." She sounded as though she were smiling too. "She doesn't quite like calling me Missus when she knows it should be Doctor, and she's a bit uncomfortable calling another lady Doctor. Using first names just makes things much easier."

Two sets of footfalls rang on the wooden floorboards, one retreating, the other drawing nearer. He caught the scent of lilies of the valley rising above the sweetness of hay from outside and forced himself to take a deep, long breath to loosen the knot in his chest.

"This is an amazing view." Her arm brushed his. "I haven't stopped to pay much attention to it, but it's perfectly pastoral, rather like something out of a Wordsworth poem."

"I confess I've never been much of a Wordsworth fan. I prefer Matthew Arnold."

"In truth, so do I. His work is much more relevant. Ah, here's our food." She moved away from him.

With a start, Nathan swung around and reached for the nearest chair, drawing it out for her and holding it until the rustle of skirts and shift of the chair told him she was seated. If nothing else, he could play the role of gentleman.

He rounded the table with the aid of one hand trailing along the backs of the other seats and drew out his own chair. No mishaps. Almost normal.

"Here you go, sir." Sally set a plate before him. "There's more on chafing dishes on the table. If Dr. Vanderleyden can help . . ." The young woman's voice trailed off.

"We can manage, Sally." Audrey filled in the silence. "Go on home to your husband. He's probably starving after a day in the fields."

"That he is." Sally laughed.

"If there's a lot of food left," Nathan said, "take it. That way you won't have to cook for him and delay things."

"Well, sir, I'm not sure Mrs. Chapman would like that."

Nathan gritted his teeth for a moment and counted to ten before speaking. "Sally, she gave us the food. That means we can do with it what we choose, and I choose to give it to you. In fact, from now on, when you cook for us, you will cook extra for your family."

"Sir, I . . . That is . . . Th-thank you." Sally retreated at a pace close to a run.

Neither Nathan nor Audrey spoke until the back door banged shut behind Sally, and her footfalls retreated down the steps of the rear porch.

"That was very generous of you, Dr. Maxwell. Your sister brought too much to eat. I think she must have intended it for Sally and her husband too."

"I don't care if she intended to feed me for a week. That young woman has been working hard and has to go home and do the same before she comes back here for the night. It doesn't seem fair." He picked up his fork, knowing beef from Corinne's kitchen would be tender enough to cut without a knife.

"That's considerate of you." Audrey's fork clinked on her plate. "Perhaps I should get her to teach me to cook." She paused. "Or Corinne's cook could teach me."

"You can't risk burning your hands." He grinned. "Or cutting them."

"That's why I never learned. And speaking of cuts . . ." She cleared her throat in an exaggerated way. "I've neglected yours."

"It's doing well."

"I'd like to look at it later."

"I can wait and go to Doc tomorrow. He should be all right by then."

"I see." Her tone held enough ice to freeze the dinner on their plates. "You'd rather go back to the man who nearly cost you one of your extremities."

"He's good when he's not suffering."

"And when he is, he's a menace. Nath—Doctor, you can't keep defending him until he hurts someone else."

"I'm supposed to turn my back on my mentor and friend so you can practice instead?" The words came out with a harshness he didn't intend. He scrambled to find the right apology.

"I offered to work with him." She spoke before Nathan could think of how to make up for his rudeness. "He would rather lose his practice or a patient, whichever comes first, than have a female doctor at his side."

"Speaking of female doctors at one's side . . ." Nathan gripped the edge of the table. "I, um, think you can ignore anything my sister said to you. She, um, worries about me too much and thinks . . . She thinks marriage is a solution to everything."

"For a woman it probably is. Being an old maid or a widow is inconvenient, at the very least."

Cutlery scraped on Audrey's plate, a sign she either continued to eat as though nothing bothered her or toyed with her food out of discomfort. A muscle jumped in Nathan's jaw as he ached to know which it was.

"Finish eating, Dr. Maxwell. It's such a lovely evening, I think we should take another walk," she continued in a calm, matter-of-fact tone.

"Yes, ma'am." He ate, though the beef and peas and potatoes may as well have been the same food with slightly different textures. He tasted nothing, and every bite settled in his stomach like a rifle cartridge. Every minute of silence between them tightened his insides so much, he thought those cartridges would combust.

As the clock in the parlor struck the quarter hour, he set down his fork and pushed back his chair. "I should go visit Ruby. I'm sure you are taking excellent care of her, but I'd like to talk to her about going to Doc's."

"She'd love a visit from you." Audrey's chair scraped. "She doesn't want to go away. She'd rather die here than leave you alone."

"I've considered moving into town, though I doubt there's a house to let."

"There aren't even any rooms to let." Audrey's voice came from higher up. She must have stood up. Dishes clattered. Footfalls sounded on the floor. "If you're finished, I can wash up here while you visit Ruby."

"I'd rather help clean up."

"You shouldn't get your hand wet."

"And you shouldn't—"

Footfalls pounded down the stairs, accompanied by the rattle of crockery. "Dr. Nathan, Ruby says I'm to clean these here dishes up." James clattered into the kitchen. "She says if either of you argues, she's coming down herself."

"She's feeling much better then." Nathan couldn't help but smile. "I'm glad to hear it."

"Yes, sir, she's nearly her old self." James sounded joyful. "But she'd love to see you, sir."

"He was just on his way up," Audrey said. "I'll help you, Mr. Buck."

"No, ma'am, you go sit down." James' tone was firm. "You're looking peaky."

"She sounds peaky," Nathan added, as he headed for the steps.

He would let Audrey tussle with James on her own. Fighting either him or Ruby was usually a lost cause.

Smiling, Nathan reached Ruby's sickroom and tapped on the door. Her command to enter indeed sounded like the woman who had raised him from the time his mother died when he was ten, then bullied him into doing as much for himself as he could after he returned to the farm to heal in spirit if not in body.

"It's about time you got up here," she greeted him. "Thought you could forget about me, did you, and leave me in the hands of that young woman calling herself a doctor?"

"She is a doctor." Nathan approached the bed and held out his hand. "She may have had a better medical education than I had."

"Humph." Ruby clasped his hand in both of hers. Her skin was dry and wrinkled over her protuberant knuckles but not feverishly hot. "Nobody's as good a doctor as you."

"As I was." Nathan listened for wheezing in Ruby's breathing and breathed a silent sigh of relief when he heard next to none. "Doc was always the best doctor I knew, even if he chose to practice in a rural county instead of the city."

"He ain't so good no more, though." Ruby sniffed.

"He is." Nathan thought of the perfect stitches Doc had managed. "We just have to keep him on the straight and narrow. And that's what I want you to help me with. Will you do it? You need to live in town, and there isn't anywhere else but his place. And if anyone can keep him sober and concentrating on his work, it's you. You can also make sure his patients come back to him so he can rebuild his practice."

"You trying to get rid of me?" Ruby's tone held a note of hurt. "All that flattery while you're telling me to go work for someone else?"

"No, Ruby, I'm trying to keep you. You can come back in the winter." He groped behind him with his foot, found a chair, and sat. "These attacks are getting more frequent, Ruby. This was a bad one. It could have killed you. Another one might."

"That's what Dr. Audrey says." Ruby heaved a gusty sigh, coughed, and removed her hand from Nathan's. "But I can't leave you. Who'll take care of you?"

"Sally will cook for me. We've settled that."

"And in-between times? I know James and I aren't educated, but we can do some reading for you and take you for walks."

"You make me sound like a lap dog."

"Humph. You're trying to take my mind in another direction."

"All right. All right." Nathan sighed this time. "I can move in with Corinne. My nephews will drive me a little crazy, but if it's the only way to get you to move into town, then I'll do it."

"There is another way." Ruby chuckled. "You could ma—"

"Don't say it." Nathan flung up one hand. "She's only been a widow for four months. In no way can she be interested in marrying someone else. She'll go home to her family."

"From what James says, that ain't such a good idea for her. He says they'll make her sit around and do nothing and never be a doc like she wants to be. And you wouldn't stop her, would you?"

"I . . . don't know."

Nathan shifted on the chair, wishing he knew the room so he could walk around and not worry about tripping over things. He always liked to walk when he needed to puzzle something out. Not being free to do so sometimes left him feeling like standing on the front porch and howling like the foxes in the woods.

"I don't know," he repeated.

He imagined Audrey going off to help some sick or injured person or a lady in labor while he remained home with little or nothing to do.

As Ruby lay quietly in her sickbed and the first cicadas of the evening began their chorus in the trees, he thought about Audrey, capable and highly trained, sitting home with little or nothing to do.

"If you want to marry her," Ruby said in a low voice, "you gotta let her do her work. It mayn't be quite right for a lady to be doctoring folks, but she's got a way about her even Doc never had when he was at his best."

"She's better off going home to her family." Nathan stood. "And you need your rest if you're going to be moving into town tomorrow."

"Dr. Nathan—"

"Good night, Ruby." Before she could say anything else, he exited the chamber and headed downstairs.

Chatter, the splash of water, and the clink of dishes in the kitchen told him Audrey was helping James with the clearing up and talking with him while they were at it. For several minutes, Nathan stood in the doorway between the kitchen and dining room and listened to Audrey's smooth voice describing that monstrous new structure in Paris named the Eiffel Tower after its engineer.

"Why would anyone want to go and make something like that?" James asked.

"Because they could?" Audrey chuckled.

The mere sound made Nathan smile.

"Truth to tell, Mr. Buck," she added, "it is a fascinating sight. All that steel soaring into the air."

"Huh." A dish thunked onto the work space. "That's the last of the dishes, ma'am. Thank you for your help."

"Thank you for letting me help you. I've been too idle of late. I—Oh, Dr. Maxwell, I didn't hear you come in."

"I was listening to your tales of Paris' latest eyesore. I'd love to climb it one day."

"There are a lot of steps." Cloth snapped in the air. "Mr. Buck, will you take this cloth to the clothesline on your way home?"

"Yes, ma'am." James made no movement toward the door. "I guess I should start packing my Ruby's things."

"We do have to ask Doc about her staying there first," Nathan pointed out. "We'll go in, in the morning, and talk to him."

"Yes, sir." The floorboards creaked as James shifted from foot to foot. "Do you want me to take you for a walk, Dr. Nathan?"

"I was rather hoping Dr. Vanderleyden would accompany me." Nathan turned his face in the direction from which he had last heard Audrey's voice. "If you're not too tired, Doctor."

"Not at all. It's a fine, cool evening after such a hot day." Her voice grew louder as she approached him.

"That be August here in the mountains," James said, turning away. "Cools off right fine at night. I'll see y'all in the morning, then, if you don't need anything else."

"Thank you, no." Nathan held out his hand.

As he hoped she would, Audrey took it and tucked it into the crook of her elbow. "Let's go in the opposite direction from where we went earlier so we don't have the setting sun in our eyes." She headed for the door. "I mean, so I don't—" She broke off with a little gulp.

"It's all right." He patted her arm. "That sort of thing doesn't offend me. Besides, I can feel the sun and remember."

They reached the door. With his long arms he managed to stretch past her and push it open, then hold it for her. If nothing else, he could still be a gentleman.

He just hadn't been gentleman enough not to walk away when he knew his sister intended to mention marriage. Audrey was so much a lady, she chose to ignore the incident. Good. He couldn't let her marry him, be responsible for him, be his companion, provide him with conversation, and read to him in that lovely voice simply because he wanted it.

That was why he hadn't stopped Corinne.

They needed to talk about it and clear the air between them. Of course, she intended to leave in a day or two. No, tomorrow. She would have to leave when Ruby left or create a worse scandal than their being alone together in the hotel room. Only her leaving town would stop tongues wagging on that score. Her leaving or marrying him.

Talk. He must talk to her about it.

The rhythm of their matching footfalls emphasized his inability to speak on the topic uppermost in his mind. In August, few birds sang in the evening, and cows and sheep in nearby pastures were settled for the night. Between the waves of the cicada chorus, a light breeze stirred the trees with a rustling swish similar to Audrey's skirts.

"I'll miss you if you leave." The words sprang from him as unplanned as a thunderstorm sweeping over the mountains. He tried to counter his outburst. "That is, when you leave. If Ruby leaves tomorrow, you won't have any choice, and—"

"Nathan." Her use of his first name was like soothing salve on a wound. "We can talk about what Corinne— Oh, I am sorry. I should have called you Dr. Maxwell. How forward of me. We really do have manners up north and—"

"Shh." Laughing, Nathan stopped on the side of the road and turned to face her. The sound of her low chuckle gave him the guidance he needed to rest his hand against her cheek. "I love my sister dearly. She doesn't have a mean bone in her body. But she can be more than a little managing."

"It's obvious she means well." Audrey didn't try to move her head away from his touch. She stood motionless. Perhaps too motionless.

Nathan allowed his fingertips to take in the smooth curve of her cheek, then lowered his hand to his side. "We planned to make you want to leave. Doc was doing better with his problem, and your being around upset him. So Corinne telegraphed your mother and mother-in-law, hoping they would persuade you to go home. But you're pretty determined."

"Considering what I had to do to get through medical training, did you think I'd give up so easily?" Frustration rang in her voice. "Yes, the Vanderleydens are rich, and my parents are more than comfortable, but Adam and I used up almost all our savings and all his allowance when we bought the practice. The allowance ended with his death. It'll start up again if I deliver a boy, in which case the Vanderleydens will accept him as an heir. I needed the income from the practice. I could have done well even working with Doc." She resumed walking, faster this time. "Corinne said she'd help me if Doc would let me work with him, but she must have known he wouldn't."

"Wouldn't you think less of us if we didn't give our loyalty to someone we've known all our lives?"

"You haven't done much for him in the past two years."

Nathan turned his face away from her. "To my shame, I've only been thinking of myself. I needed specialists and so got all my doctoring in Baltimore."

"I'm sorry." She covered his hand where it rested on her arm. "You seem to have adjusted so well, I'm not thinking how much your own life has been disrupted."

"It's no excuse for being a selfish beast." Nathan tried to smile. "Helping Doc recover is the least I can do for all he's done for me in the past."

"Of course it is." She squeezed his hand and released it. "And I couldn't be responsible for his relapse, which is why I decided to leave until—" She snapped her teeth together as though biting off her statement.

"Until he made a mess of my hand," Nathan supplied.

"It did make me reconsider the wisdom of leaving an entire

county in the hands of a man like that." She slowed to a leisurely pace again. "Doctors are supposed to do no harm."

"I'm hoping that, by living there, Ruby can keep him on the straight and narrow." Nathan sighed. "It may be useless, but I have to try."

"If you and Corinne are so devoted to restoring Dr. Hornsby to his former glory, why would she . . ." She took a deep breath. "Why would she suggest I marry you?"

"And why wouldn't I stop her?" He spoke the unasked part of the question. "I should think it obvious."

Her arm tensed beneath his fingers. "I'm not a nurse."

"No, you're not. You're a great deal more."

More than he was willing to admit to her for fear of scaring her off.

"I had nurses right after my accident," he plunged on. "But they got bored here in the country, and finding ones who were competent and good companions was almost impossible. Since I sent the last one packing who thought she could steal from me since I couldn't see, Corinne has been trying to find me a wife. But no one is that desperate."

"And you think I am?" A stone rattled along the road with so much force, he suspected she'd kicked it.

"I think we could be of mutual benefit to each other." He chose his remarks with care. "I don't expect more. I know you're still grieving your husband, so I don't expect you to . . . care deeply for me. But we seem to get on well and . . . and . . ." He didn't know what else to say.

Apparently, neither did she. As the sun fell behind the mountains, taking the heat from the day, and the cicadas fell silent, the crunch of their footfalls on the gravel became the only sound in the evening for five endless minutes.

Then she paused beside a patch of fragrant wild roses and removed her arm from beneath his hand. "I should be grieving my husband." Her muffled tone told him she had turned away from him. Foliage rustled as though she toyed with it. "I miss him. He was my best friend for most of my life. But our marriage . . ." She took a shuddering, audible breath. "We didn't have a great love other than our friendship. Adam married me because a union between us was acceptable to our families and he knew how badly I wanted to go to medical school. He married me so I could be a doctor. He could have had a conventional wife, one who loved him and was home at night when he returned from seeing patients. One who saw that the servants got everything right instead of relying on them to simply do their work without supervision. He could have had a wife who loved him devotedly . . . passionately. But he loved me so much that he wanted me to be a doctor because I wanted to be one, even though he knew I loved him as no more than a friend. So I'm under an obligation to continue my work and use my education and training. But the baby . . . Providing him with an heir was the least I could do."

"Did he know about it?" Nathan asked quietly.

"He did. It's why he made me promise not to stop practicing no matter what. But now . . . The mothers . . ." Her voice sounded muffled, as though she had covered her face with her hands. "I feel no good to anyone these days, including myself."

Nathan's heart twisted. With all his will he managed not to put his arms around her to offer comfort for the pain he heard in her voice. As a poor substitute he offered what words he could.

"I understand, Audrey. Believe me, I understand. For the past two years the only good I've done another person is to help Doc start back toward recovering from his loss."

"Because of me." She let out a humorous laugh. "How ironic."

"Irony or not"— Nathan took a deep breath—"your coming here could do more than a great deal of good. Both of us would benefit from marriage. I'd have the continued pleasure of your company, and the mothers couldn't take away your baby."

"They only threatened to take him away if I stayed here."

Her immediate response sent his heart plummeting to the center of his belly with a sickening thud.

"But you said you couldn't practice medicine if you went back to Connecticut," he pointed out. "And you were going to leave here."

"I don't have a choice." She nearly spat the words. "I have no more money." With a rustle of skirts that sent lilies-of-the-valley fragrance rising above the spicy aromas of a deep country summer, she spun to face him. "I may be an unnatural woman for wanting to continue to practice my profession despite my condition and after the baby is born, but I'm not so unnatural I would starve and make the baby suffer."

"But in returning you will break your promise to your husband."

"Yes, but I have no choice that I can see."

His heart pounding so hard he could scarcely get the words out, Nathan asked, "And if you had another choice, would you take it?"

"You mean marry you?" She, too, sounded as though speaking were difficult.

"Yes."

"Are you saying you would let me practice medicine?"

"Yes. Under one condition."

Chapter Ten

STAYING IN VIRGINIA STOP MARRIED YESTERDAY STOP

Audrey watched the telegrapher send her message. Each click of the key tapping the Morse code along the wires sounded like a slamming door, a clank far louder than the thump of the preacher closing his prayer book at the end of the brief marriage ceremony.

She was no longer Dr. Audrey Sinclair Vanderleyden. She was now Dr. Audrey Sinclair Maxwell, a bride a mere four and a half months after the death of her first husband in order to fulfill a promise and clear her conscience.

A nice sentiment except that she now felt guilty for accepting Nathan's proposal and his name.

He was getting a great deal from the marriage. Nothing about the union was one-sided on the surface. In exchange for his home and the security of being wife to a well-off man, she provided him with companionship and care. He helped her gain acceptance into the county. She ran his household. He spared her reputation. She read to him and walked with him. It was an admirable arrangement.

Or would be if she didn't suspect that he was in love with her.

"Anything else, ma'am?"

Audrey started at the sound of the telegrapher's voice.

"No, thank you." She smiled at how much more respectful he was to her now. "Thank you for sending them right away."

"Of course, ma'am." He stood, fidgeting with his tie, his heightened color rosy beneath the dandelion fluff of his hair.

"Yes?" Audrey arched her eyebrows. "May I help you with something?"

"Uh, are you still a doctor?"

"Do you mean did I stop being one because I got married?"

His Adam's apple bobbed up and down, and he nodded.

She smiled. "Yes, I'm still a doctor, though"—she winced—"my practice is limited."

"How limited?" He stared past her toward the door as though fearing someone would walk in on them.

"My husband would prefer it if I didn't interfere with Dr. Hornsby's work." She managed to keep the contempt from her tone. She didn't trust the man and wasn't certain anyone else should. "That probably means doctoring on any men."

"And rightly so. Rightly so." His head bobbed like that of a marionette with a broken string. "But this ain't for me."

"Oh?" She waited.

The Adam's apple bobbed again. "Ma'am, Dr. Ma'am, d'you think you could come visit my momma?"

"Your mother?" Audrey stared, wondering how old his mother must be since he couldn't be under sixty-five. "Is she ill?"

"Nope. Never been ill a day in all her eighty-five years, but she's got the cataracts and don't want Doc . . . Well, he used to be the best in the Shenandoah Valley for taking care of cataracts, but his hands aren't so steady nowadays. And I was thinking . . . Well, shucks, if Dr. Maxwell thinks you're all right, maybe you're good enough to see to my momma."

Audrey shuddered inside at the idea of using the couching needle on someone's eye. She knew how it was done—in theory.

She had seen it done—once. She even possessed the right instruments. But to actually shove a steel point through someone's pupil made her queasy to consider.

Not a reaction a doctor should have.

She steeled herself. "I'll . . . try." She feared her voice reflected her tremor.

"Didn't think a lady doctor could do something like that." He curled his upper lip.

"Of course I can do it." She injected hauteur into her tone. "It's just not always successful, that's all."

"Huh. Well, come on out to our house day after tomorrow. We live on Buckmarsh two blocks down from Church. All the trim's painted blue. Momma likes blue."

"Around one o'clock then."

Legs a bit rubbery, Audrey left the telegraph office. A strong breeze caught at her filmy cotton skirt, a white skirt figured with tiny blue flowers. In honor of her marriage she had set aside her blacks. Unlike her heavy mourning clothes, her summer garments, purchased before they left Paris the previous summer and let out in the waist with the aid of her one feminine skill— the ability to sew fine stitches—floated about with feminine and impractical allure.

Impractical except for now, when she used the need to tame her gown as an excuse to stop and breathe deeply in order to calm her racing heart.

Already her marriage to Nathan was working to gain her acceptance as a doctor in the community. But why did it have to be a cataract case? If it worked, she could restore much of the woman's sight. If it failed, the old lady would be completely blind, and Audrey's reputation would be worth nothing regardless of the man to whom she was married.

She would feel more confident in a potential triumph if she had another doctor with whom she could discuss the couching beforehand. Doc was certainly not interested in hearing about her work, such as it was. And Nathan? She didn't know. They certainly discussed cases they had encountered in the past. But this one . . .

Audrey ambled toward the hotel, where Nathan would meet her after going to Doc to have his stitches removed. She hoped things would go well. She didn't want Doc to fail. If he had changed his mind and wished to continue to practice medicine, that was all right. She simply wanted to practice too. She would also like a return of the money Adam and she had paid him for his practice.

Of course, now that she had married again, that money would not be hers. Nathan would have control of it. He had promised her an allowance as part of their marriage bargain, but she'd like something set aside for her child in the event it was a daughter, and if she were fortunate enough to procure patients who didn't want to go to Doc or travel to one of the cities, she would need to replenish her medical supplies like carbolic acid and bandages. Patients would surely pay her, and any money she earned would belong to her husband.

She stopped, gripping a lamppost for support while she breathed deeply and slowly, trying to dispel the panic tightening her chest. No breathing in the world was deep and slow enough to banish the proverb racing through her mind. *Marry in haste, repent at leisure.*

Surely not. Surely Nathan would not take loyalty to his old friend so far as to deny his wife the very thing he had promised her—the ability to practice medicine. He wasn't unkind. He wasn't devious.

Panic gone for the moment, she released the lamppost and started out toward the hotel again. Ahead of her, a man stepped from a furniture store doorway, leaning heavily on a cane. Glancing down to see what his malady was, she noted one foot was bandaged from the ankle to the toes. With every step, he grunted with effort or pain, and Audrey increased her pace to fall into step beside him.

"Sir, may I help you?"

"It's you." He stopped and scowled at her from beneath bushy brows. "You're that female doc who told me to stop eating red meat and drinking my homemade wine."

"For the gout, yes." She smiled at him. "Jasper. I didn't catch a last name."

"Smithfield. Like that place where they burned witches back in Queen Mary's day."

"Excuse me?"

Audrey hadn't paid much attention to her history courses. She had, however, paid attention to her medical classes, and one matter she recalled was that no one with gout would be able to stand the sort of bandaging Jasper Smithfield sported on his affected toe.

"Has the diet change helped?" she asked.

"Nope. Didn't do a bit of good." He curled his upper lip. "Those fancy schools don't teach you all anything, do they? Keeping a man from his good food for nothing. And I couldn't sit around anymore, so I wrapped it up and came out to do my shopping."

"Does the bandage help?" From the corner of her eye, Audrey noticed people stopped to stare at her and Mr. Smithfield, and someone inside the store stood with his face pressed to the front window. "That's odd for gout. I'd really like to—" She sighed. "You should have Dr. Hornsby take a look at this."

"Nope. Won't. Decided you're all quacks." Smacking his cane tip against the sidewalk, he limped forward.

Audrey fell into pace beside him. "Mr. Smithfield, will you let me look at that toe? No charge, of course."

"Nope. A female doctor's a worse quack than the men." He

batted at her blowing skirt with his cane. "Move along. You're getting in my way."

"What if I tell you I'm not certain you have gout at all?"

He stopped at the foot of the hotel steps and stared at her. "Then I'd think you were as crazy as you are quacky."

"But if you have gout—"

She caught sight of James and Nathan coming across the street, the latter's left hand free of bandages, and the thought occurred to her how undignified she looked trying to chase down a patient.

"Suit yourself." She offered Jasper Smithfield her hand. "If I'm right, just keep those bandages on it, elevate the foot whenever you can, and your toe should heal in another month or so."

He narrowed his eyes at her. "What're you thinking?"

"That you have a simple break. Good afternoon, Nathan. I was just talking to Mr. Smithfield here."

"So I noticed." Nathan held out his hand.

Smithfield shook it but seemed suddenly tongue-tied.

"He was just telling me all doctors are quacks." Audrey spoke a bit too quickly.

"Except for you, sir," Smithfield muttered.

"I should think not." Nathan laughed. "Neither is Dr. Hornsby."

Audrey winced.

"Or my wife," he added as though in an afterthought.

"Your wife?" Smithfield stared from Nathan to Audrey. "You aren't so ill that you need a doc around all the time, are you?"

"I'm as healthy as a horse." Nathan flashed Audrey a smile that curled her toes. "But I had to find a way to keep her around."

"I don't know, Dr. Maxwell." Smithfield shook his head. "She might be pretty, but she's kind of forward to be a good wife. You might have trouble reining her in."

"I can manage her." Nathan's eyes danced.

Audrey ground her teeth. "I am not a recalcitrant filly."

The men laughed. Smithfield slapped Nathan on the back and hobbled off.

"I hope it is gout," Audrey muttered.

"It isn't?" Nathan's eyebrows went up.

"He has it wrapped tightly. I don't think he could bear the pressure on it if it were gout."

"A break then." A light sparked in Nathan's eyes, a dance of excitement. "I wish— Well, would you like some lemonade before we head home?"

"I'd rather go home."

Odd how easily she used that word already. But the farmhouse felt like home, cozy, inviting, and filled with the rich aromas of peaches and early apples from the orchard that Sally and her mother were canning. Audrey wanted to taste those peaches and apples, perhaps have tea with a slice of pie if they'd baked the one they'd promised, and talk to Nathan about the couching. They couldn't discuss medical issues in the hotel dining room.

"Are you tired?" Nathan looked concerned. "Was everything all right at the telegraph office?"

"Yes, the telegrapher couldn't have been more polite." She frowned. "I don't know his name."

"Wilson. Harold Wilson." He turned. "James, will you get the carriage?"

"Yes, sir." He headed down Church Street.

Audrey took Nathan's left hand in hers. "It looks quite well."

With the exception of the bigger-than-necessary scar.

"Is Dr. Hornsby doing well? And Ruby?"

"Ruby is doing very well. Nothing she likes better than having someone she can boss around."

"You weren't enough?"

"I've got you now." He curled his fingers around hers.

A middle-aged lady passing by gave them a disgusted glance. She looked like one of the women who had objected to her doctoring Nathan in the hotel room. Audrey considered flashing her wedding ring in the woman's face but realized it would do no good. She'd been wearing a wedding band that day too. She doubted the woman would notice the difference between the two gold bands.

The difference lay on the inside. The one now suspended from a gold chain around her neck had been engraved with the initials *ASV* twice with the symbol for eternity between them. The ring now gracing Audrey's left-hand ring finger bore no carving or markings to state eternal connection and devotion.

Twice now she had married without mutual love. Once again she had married for what the man could give her with too little in return from her.

She removed her hand from Nathan's and put a pace of distance between them. "We're blocking the steps."

Not really. People could get around them, not that anyone had wanted to.

Nathan closed his eyes for a moment, opened his mouth as though intending to speak, then closed it again and turned toward the rumble of carriage wheels on the brick street. It wasn't theirs, and it trundled past and turned down Main Street, the horse sweating as though it had traveled a long way quickly, the top of the buggy up, concealing the identity of the occupant.

"They shouldn't drive that fast in town," Nathan said.

"They're stopping at Dr. Hornsby's." Audrey stepped to the curb for a better look. "Yes, a man and a woman are carrying a child inside. I should go—" She bit her lip and turned away. "I hope it's nothing serious."

"He can manage it."

"Of course."

To her relief, James pulled up then. Audrey climbed into the landaulet without assistance and settled on the forward-facing seat. She left enough room for Nathan, but he chose to sit across from her.

They certainly didn't look like a newlywed couple. They

looked like mere acquaintances. More than one passerby gave them curious glances. No doubt most people in town knew they were married. People would expect them to act like newly-weds.

Well, when had she ever acted the way others expected her to?

Yet she felt unbalanced without Nathan seated beside her. And foolish. She should have seated herself in the middle if he weren't going to join her.

Much ado about nothing. Truly. If he chose to be uncomfortable, it was none of her concern. He was a grown man and capable of making his own decisions. Just because his sister tried to manage his life, just because Ruby had told him when to rise, eat, and go to bed didn't mean she should, simply because she was his wife. This was a marriage of convenience. They had both agreed to that. No love. No deep, emotional ties to one another. They merely joined her name to his to give her shelter, provide him with a companion, and help her to keep her baby without the strictures of living with her mother or mother-in-law. She should be happy about all that. Nathan should be happy about all that.

He looked as sad as she felt. The rumbling wheels over rough roads and whoosh of wind through the tree branches overhead made the silence between Audrey and Nathan more profound. Gripping the edge of the seat, she strove to find some conversational gambit.

"I've been asked to see a patient," she blurted out. "I mean, a potential patient."

"Oh?" Nathan faced her but showed no curiosity.

"Mrs. Wilson. The telegrapher's mother. I presume she's Mrs. Wilson."

"She is." Now interest sparked in his eyes, a curious thing when she remembered he couldn't see a thing. "Why does she need care? She thinks herself the best apothecary in the county and then some." He grinned. "Fortunately she is rather good at dosing herself, since she's had to give herself a couple of antidotes upon occasion."

"How do you know?" Audrey leaned toward him. "Mr. Wilson said she's never been to a doctor."

"She hasn't, but she tells people, who tells others . . ." He shrugged. "Nothing remains a secret for long in this little county."

"I suppose not. I've never lived in a place with so few people."

"And many around here think it's too crowded. But do tell."

"I think it's cataracts."

"Cataracts!" His knuckles whitened over the arm of the seat. "Surely you don't have the experience to handle a couching needle."

"I haven't done it before, but I've seen it done."

"She should go to Doc. He's done it often. I'll tell him—"

"That he should take a patient from me?" Audrey knew her voice rose and didn't care. "Do you want a poor, half-blind old lady to go to Doc with his unsteady hands and have him shove a needle through her pupil?"

Nathan whitened.

The speeding carriage swept down a hill, and Audrey's stomach lurched.

"I-I'm s-sorry." She managed to stammer out an apology, though she wasn't quite certain for what.

"No need." Nathan rubbed the side of his head.

Although a wave of golden brown hair covered each temple, Audrey guessed at the scars there, where the small pistol ball had passed right through his skull. A fraction of an inch to the right or left, up or down, and he would be dead. She had never heard of such a bizarre occurrence as the optic nerves being severed by a single shot without any other damage. Apparently it happened. His eyes were still intact, but the nerves that went from the eyes to the brain made a person see, and without them one couldn't.

Nathan couldn't, and the world had lost a fine doctor. Worse, perhaps, Nathan had lost his profession.

Still on the brink of losing hers, Audrey understood his regret.

"Nathan." She reached across the carriage and gripped his hand, though it made her balance precariously on the seat. "I would like your help if she agrees to go along with this procedure."

"I don't know how I can help." The way his face brightened belied his words.

"Have you ever done a couching?"

"Twice, before I settled on obstetrics."

"Then give me every detail. Please."

"Let me remember here. . . ." He made a great show of thinking, tilting his face toward the heavy clouds darkening the sky, pursing his lips and steepling his fingers beneath his chin.

Audrey waited, a smile curving her lips.

"It was the oddest thing," he intoned like a poet about to recite. "The woman was quite young. Sixteen or seventeen. Far too young to have cataracts, but there they were . . ."

He talked on, and Audrey listened, enthralled. Entranced. Until that moment she hadn't quite realized what a fine voice he possessed, deep without being heavy and with the lightest hint of his Virginia-mountain heritage adding warmth and color. It was a voice one could listen to for hours.

She did listen to him for hours. From the couching procedures they moved on to other medical incidents they had encountered, oddities and possible causes or cures. A storm kept her from going into town the next day, so she pulled medical journals from the shelves in the room that her mother would have called a library and Nathan called his den.

They talked of little else. He was more like a close colleague than a husband. She felt as though history repeated itself.

Heavyhearted with the thought, she prepared to go into town the next morning and encountered a difficulty she determined to solve at once. With James living in town now, they had no one to drive the carriage. They didn't even have the carriage.

But they did have more horses. Nathan admitted that he planned on riding again so kept his riding stock. In addition he kept an extra carriage team. Sometimes they were employed for light farmwork, as they could pull a wagon.

"Then they can pull a governess cart too. Or one of them can," Audrey pointed out. "Do you have one?"

"No, but Corinne does." Nathan frowned. "I'm sure she's not using it now, but you can't either."

"Why not? I know how to drive. And it's perfectly safe."

"You shouldn't be, though."

"No, I should impose on James?" Audrey crossed her arms over her chest. "What if there's an emergency? What if someone needs me to help? Am I supposed to walk into town and fetch James? Or wake one of the farmworkers to take me in a wagon? How is that safer?"

Nathan laughed. "No, you're right. I simply worry about you. Audrey, you're in a delicate condition."

"There is nothing delicate about me." She laughed, too, and wanted to hug him.

She liked someone worrying about her. As long as that worry didn't keep her bound to a farm about which she knew nothing that she had any reason to learn.

"I'm an excellent driver," she wheedled gently. "You can have James judge me on that."

"I'll have James find the slowest pony in our stock." He sighed. "I understand how you feel about staying here all the time with too little to occupy your time."

Her heart went out to him. She knew he fretted over not being able to mow hay or plow fields. The farm consisted of four hundred acres of hay, dairy cattle, and orchards. The land had been in the Maxwell family for a hundred and fifty years, so Nathan had kept it after he'd gone to the city to become a doctor. He hadn't returned except for occasional holidays. Once a week Nathan and James went over the accounts, the former calculating in his mind with a speed and accuracy that boggled Audrey's mind. Other than that he left the day-to-day operations to his capable manager.

And Nathan was bored, as Audrey knew she would be if forced to remain in a home where she had little to do, since housework and cooking had not been part of her privileged upbringing. Realizing the depth of his ennui, Audrey began to suspect that what she had feared was too much attraction to her merely stemmed from an eagerness for the companionship of someone who understood the thing that interested him most—medicine.

Because he had done so much for her, she tried to return the favor and alleviate his boredom. For her next medical call she invited him to go with her in the cart he had so kindly provided. "It's old Mrs. Wilson."

"If she didn't want Doc," he protested, "she sure won't want me."

"There's no connection there." Audrey laid his coat across his arm. "Come along, unless you don't trust my driving."

"James says you're as good as you say you are, so I trust you."

"Then come."

He went. Mrs. Wilson, tiny without being frail, greeted them with vigorous handshakes and the squinted eyes of someone trying to see.

"This cataract is unsightly," she declared before they were over the threshold. "Can you fix it? If you can't, then say so, and I'll resign myself to getting Harold to read to me, bad at it as he is."

"I think I can fix it."

Even before Nathan squeezed her elbow, Audrey knew she shouldn't have expressed herself with doubt.

"Usually it can be fixed," she corrected herself. "Your sight won't be perfect, but it will improve."

"Heh. We'll see about that." Mrs. Wilson let them in.

Audrey examined the eye, told the old lady precisely what she had to do, and tried to give her time to think about it.

"Nope, do it right now," was the response.

Audrey wished *she* had time to think about it. Dry-mouthed, her heart racing, she took Mrs. Wilson to her bedchamber and made her preparations, then returned downstairs to find Nathan sipping tea in the parlor.

"I want you to talk me through this," she announced.

"You know what to do." He sat motionless, his head bent.

"Then be someone I can talk to. Please."

"All right." His knuckles were white on his cup.

She led him upstairs and narrated every step she took.

If done right, the procedure in truth produced little pain for the patient. The pain, Audrey decided at the end, went to the doctor, whose muscles were as tense as telegraph wires.

"I want you to rest for a week." She tied a patch over the affected eye. "I mean true rest. Stay in your bed."

"Nothing will get done if I do."

"Nothing will get done if you don't."

Needing to get away before her knees gave way, Audrey summoned the Wilsons' maid to sit with the old lady and guided Nathan back to the governess cart.

"Are you all right?" He slipped his arm around her waist.

Conscious of being on a main thoroughfare, she refrained from leaning against him. "I will be. I think it was successful. What do you think from what I was saying?"

He said nothing for so long, she feared he disapproved of her procedure, or her manner with the patient, or her work altogether. She had driven the cart well out of town before he spoke.

"I think you are an excellent doctor."

The praise warmed her, releasing the last of her tension. Yet despite his approval he wouldn't return to Mrs. Wilson's for a follow-up examination. Nor did he go with her when a neighbor asked her to tend to a sick child or when one of the farmworkers received a serious cut from a scythe.

She didn't mind Nathan's not joining her. Their time together was otherwise enjoyable, whether on long walks along the road or through the orchards and woods, or reading novels or poetry in the shade of a walnut tree. But lately Nathan seemed disinterested in hearing the details of her work, and when a friend from medical school sent her a parcel with several issues of the British medical journal *The Lancet,* Nathan didn't want her to read them to him.

But he went into town with James on several occasions to visit Doc.

"He's doing very well," he told her after the third such call at the end of August. "Ruby makes sure he is well fed, and having her around seems to attract patients. Of course, she feeds them cookies when they come."

"Any serious cases?" Audrey wanted to know out of professional curiosity, not nosiness.

Nathan merely shrugged. "Your coming here has been a good thing for all of us."

"I'm glad you think so." Her tone was less than friendly, and she exited to the front porch before she said something she would regret.

That didn't stop her from thinking of how Nathan was keeping her out of professional talk. He had wanted to hear about medical things from her until he actually saw her successfully perform a procedure.

For a moment her mind flashed back to her first week at the New York Infirmary. A difficult delivery requiring a caesarian. Two doctors in the ward—she and Adam. She'd performed the surgery. Adam, who had a sprained thumb and couldn't, didn't attend the delivery. He didn't even want to hear about how the procedure went.

She bowed her head and covered her face with her hands. All she ever wanted was to be a doctor. She'd been happy to marry Adam because she loved him as a friend and rather liked many aspects of marriage. She'd grieved the loss of their friendship long before he died and had wondered how many years of their steadily cooling relationship she could bear. Her work at the infirmary helped.

So why, when she had gotten herself into a similar situation, did her chest ache at Nathan's lack of interest in her work?

"Audrey?" Nathan's voice resounded through the front door a moment before it opened.

Footfalls thudded on the wooden planks. She waited, expecting him to stop, to ask her where she was. But he came straight to her and touched her arm.

"Are you all right?" Gently, he tugged her hand from her face. "Did I say something wrong?"

"How did you find me?" she couldn't help asking.

He grinned. "Your scent. Lilies of the valley."

"I'll have to change it if I need to hide from you." She felt a little breathless.

"And remain silent and still. I can pick your voice from half a dozen others, and I recognize your walk."

"And you're not pretending you can't see?" She smiled, hoping he would understand she was teasing him.

"I wish I were."

"No, I'm sorry. It was thoughtless—"

"Shh." He laid his finger across her lips. "I apparently have said something I shouldn't."

"No, Nathan, it's what you haven't said that hurts me."

She had nothing to lose by being honest and perhaps something to gain.

"You spend hours with Doc, presumably talking about his cases, but you don't want to know a thing about mine."

"I know." He held her hand between both of his, the scar on his left palm rough against her fingers. "But it's not because I don't care. It's just that . . . Audrey, I'd like us to have something else to share besides medicine. You said that's all you had between you and your first husband. . . ." He trailed off but released her fingers and cupped her face in his hands.

She stood gazing up at him, speechless, beginning to understand.

He closed his eyes, and she caught her breath, quite certain, anticipating—

Galloping hooves thundered along the drive. Audrey sprang away from Nathan, her cheeks heating.

A youth astride a lovely black horse reined in at the foot of the steps. "Got a letter for Dr. Maxwell. The lady doc, that is."

"A letter?" Audrey's heart galloped like the black horse inside her chest. "Bad news?"

Controlling the hard-breathing mount with his knees, the youth doffed his hat with one hand and retrieved a letter from his coat pocket with the other.

"A letter, not a telegram?" Audrey descended the steps, holding out her hand for the missive. "From whom?"

She need not have asked. The crest in the corner told her.

"What is it?" Nathan asked.

"It's from Tom Buress, my attorney." She tore open the envelope. "It's . . . It's not an emergency. He's simply telling me the judge is back in town and wishes to meet with me tomorrow."

Chapter Eleven

Getting married again had been a mistake. As much as she liked, admired, and felt for her husband, she never understood the full implication of being a married woman until she sat beside her attorney, Tom Buress, and heard the judge's decision.

"But I'm Adam's heir. Nathan isn't."

Her outburst was hushed but loud enough for everyone in the courtroom to turn and stare at her. The judge glared. Dr. Hornsby smirked. Nathan, seated on her other side, reached out and squeezed her hand. His chiseled lips tightened at the corners, and his eyes remained devoid of expression.

Judge Bennett's eyes remained anything but expressionless. Those black orbs glowed like burning coals in the middle of his suntanned and wrinkled face as he glowered down at her. "Young lady, you should consider yourself blessed that two men have been willing to marry you and take care of you. Now go home and live up to the role you should be playing, that of wife and mother."

"But—"

Buress' hand gripped her arm, reminding her to keep her mouth shut. One did not argue with a judge.

She hung her head in pretended humility and acquiescence. Inside, her stomach boiled over with resentment like an angry creature about to emerge from a swamp. She gritted her teeth to stop an outraged flow of words.

"All rise." The bailiff dismissed the courtroom.

Audrey thought she would burst before she got outside into the clear light of a September afternoon. Her jaw ached from keeping her mouth shut, and bile burned in her throat.

"Come to my office." Buress gripped her elbow on one side, Nathan on the other. "We can talk freely there."

"This isn't justice." Audrey's eyes brimmed with tears, and she blinked hard to keep them from rolling down her cheeks. "A man to take care of me. I'm the one who—"

She snapped her teeth together again. Never could she be so unkind as to declare in front of Nathan, or to anyone, that she was the one who took care of her husbands. Adam would never have gotten through medical school without her tutelage. Nathan . . .

She doubted he needed any help getting through anything in his life until the accident. His was the most competent medical mind she'd ever encountered. He also needed no help in taking care of himself. He simply couldn't read or go for walks on his own. Well, farmwork was probably out, and she didn't think anyone wanted him driving or wielding a scythe.

And he couldn't practice medicine.

When Nathan told her he understood how she felt about no longer being able to practice, she believed he was sincere. He couldn't practice, and her heart broke for him each time she saw his fingers curl as though he were holding a scalpel or a needle, each time his face lit up when he argued about the conclusions of a writer in a medical journal.

Empathy or not, Audrey didn't want to find herself in his position simply for being a woman.

"I know the judge knows more about the law than I do," Audrey couldn't stop herself from saying, a block from the office. "But I don't see how he can possibly be right."

"I agree with you." Buress gave his response in the two minutes it took them to reach his office. "As far as I'm concerned, your claim is clear." He unlocked his door. "Come in."

Once they were all seated, he ensconced himself behind his wide desk and drummed his fingers on the surface as he glanced from Nathan to Audrey. "You can appeal to a higher court."

"I can?" Audrey leaned forward, realizing as she did so that her expanding tummy tugged at her clothes. "How? Where?"

"Well . . ." Buress settled his gaze on Nathan. "We need your husband's permission to do so."

"But it's my case," Audrey protested.

"Dr. Maxwell?" Buress asked.

Nathan shifted on his chair, stretching out his long legs, bumping the soles of his shoes on the front of the desk and yanking his legs back again before he sat up straight and gripped the arms of his seat. "No, I don't think it's worth the expense and effort for what will probably not be a more favorable ruling."

"What?" Audrey turned on him, her face heating. "You want me to get cheated out of what is rightfully mine?"

"You aren't being cheated," Buress and Nathan said together.

Audrey glared at them. "It was my husband's money that bought the practice. It was our signatures on the contract. It is partly my medical degree that gave me the right to work with my husband. How can you say I'm not being cheated?"

"Calm yourself, Audrey." Nathan leaned toward her and rested his hand on the arm of her chair. "My dear, it's not good for you or the baby."

"The judge has ordered Dr. Hornsby to pay you back the money with interest," Buress pointed out.

"He has ordered Dr. Hornsby to pay Nathan back the money." Audrey feared she was going to cry from rage and frustration. "It's not my money now; it's Nathan's."

This was why she shouldn't have married. If only she had been able to hold on for two more weeks, she would have been able perhaps to borrow money on the claim of her money coming from Dr. Hornsby. That is, if anyone had been willing to lend her the funds, which, when she thought about it for a moment, seemed unlikely.

"If Nathan chooses not to accept any funds from Dr. Hornsby," she plunged on, "he doesn't have to. It's Nathan's debt to accept or reject."

Nathan removed his hand from her chair and straightened himself again, his face expressionless.

Buress cleared his throat. "Doc must pay back the money or be in contempt of court."

"Yes, and Nathan can turn around and give the money right back to him instead of to me." Audrey feared she sounded like a petulant child, but she couldn't help herself. "It's my inheritance."

"You chose to wed Dr. Maxwell." Buress gave her a sympathetic smile. "Of course I don't think that was an unwise decision on your part at all. He's not going to let you starve by any means, and you can still practice medicine."

"Except all my fees belong to my husband."

She wanted to put her head down on Buress' desk and weep.

"I have no intention of keeping your fees." Nathan's voice was strangled. "If you would like Mr. Buress to write up a contract to that effect right now, we can have him do so."

"I'll have to do research as to the legal implications of that," Buress said. "But if it would make you feel better, Dr. Vander— er, Dr. Maxwell, I can go ahead."

"I'd rather"— Nathan cleared his throat—"she trusted my word."

Audrey's heart skipped a beat. She looked at him, read misery on his face, and realized how unkind she had been to him in the past quarter hour. At the least she had said "my husband" to refer to Adam, who was not her present husband. Adam who, like a spoiled child, had gone boating when warned not to and gotten himself killed.

Nathan, like the kind and generous man he was, was giving her a measure of freedom few married women enjoyed.

"Nathan, I-I—" Her throat closed.

"I'll fetch us some tea." Buress rose and headed toward a door at the back of his office.

"Audrey." Nathan reached toward her again. He touched her arm and traced his fingers down her sleeve until he reached her hand, clasping it with warm, strong fingers. "Audrey, I didn't marry you to stop you from practicing medicine. I told you that, when we made our arrangement. You are free to take any patients who want to come to you instead of Doc."

"Women and children," Audrey interjected but without her earlier peevishness.

Nathan laced his fingers with hers. "I'm sorry that's the situation you're in."

"Why would you be sorry?" Audrey couldn't stop herself from squeezing back, emphasizing the connection between them. "You didn't make the judge's decision for him."

"No, but—" He turned his face away from her as though reading the diplomas hanging on Buress' wall. "It was the incident in the hotel room. If I hadn't gone to you there—"

"You would have likely lost your hand."

"Yes, but I may have lost you your suit. That is, a couple of the old biddies who took exception to your being alone with me wrote to the judge because they know him socially, and they told him it's indecent for a woman to be treating men. They used that incident as an example."

"Oh." She felt sick. "I still would do it all over again." She turned his hand over and smoothed the scar with her fingers. "You need your hands, though I'd rather you didn't take up carving again."

"I hate leaving a job unfinished."

"Maybe a softer wood? Or sandstone? Something that isn't in need of a knife quite so sharp?"

"Maybe you could only manage cuts and bruises on children, and an occasional normal delivery, instead of cataract surgery on old ladies?"

"You drive your point home, Dr. Maxwell." She rubbed the ball of her thumb on the palm of his hand, and, her insides feeling like warm toffee, she raised his hand to her lips and kissed the scar. "Just don't drive your point into yourself again."

"Thank you for your advice, Dr. Maxwell." He caressed her cheek and smiled at her.

Audrey's mouth went dry. And in that moment only one thought ran through her head. Marrying Nathan Maxwell hadn't been a mistake after all.

"Thank you," she murmured.

"For what?"

Buress' reappearance with a tea tray prevented Audrey from answering. Accompanied by shortbread and fragrant Earl Grey, the conversation shifted from Audrey's plans to build a practice for women and children, if that was all she could manage, to Nathan's current occupation.

"I'm seeing how many books I can read in a year." Nathan spoke with a flippant edge to his tone and a shrug of his broad shoulders. "Or my wife can read to me."

"He's fibbing a bit." Audrey smiled. "He has been, I suspect, acting as a consulting colleague to Dr. Hornsby."

"And to you?" Buress pressed.

Audrey glanced from Nathan, whose face appeared a bit tight, to the attorney. "Sometimes." Afraid Buress would think this meant Nathan didn't care about her work, she hastened to add, "The only patient I've had who was a real challenge to my skill."

"You're lucky to have his knowledge then." Buress returned her smile.

"I am lucky to have his wisdom and his name." Audrey rose. "And I am also lucky to be able to pay you your full fee."

She settled her account with Buress from the fee Mrs. Wilson had paid her for the cataract surgery, then offered Nathan her arm.

Nathan said nothing as they made their way to the corner, where James waited with the carriage, but he held her arm with his hand tucked snugly against her side. And he was smiling.

Other than inconsequential talk of plans for the rest of the day and to accept a dinner invitation to Corinne and Russell Chapman's the following week, they said nothing personal until they sat alone on the porch, a book as yet unopened on Audrey's lap and a pitcher of lemonade cloudy with condensation on the table between them. As Audrey ruffled the pages of the novel, trying to find the place where they had left off the day before, Nathan held up one hand in a gesture asking for her to wait.

"Is it true, Audrey?" He drummed his long fingers on his lap. "Do you—can you possibly feel lucky you're married to me?"

"I—" Audrey let the book fall into her lap again, tried to speak twice, took a swallow of the tart-sweet lemonade, and plunged in with the truth. "When the judge gave his ruling, I thought I'd made a huge mistake. I felt like I had done all the work—and Adam, too, for that matter—and you and Doc would reap the benefits." Seeing a white line form around his mouth, she raced on. "But when you assured me you wanted me to have all the fees I earned and wouldn't stop me from seeing patients . . . Well, I added that with your generosity in marrying me and our getting on well and . . . In short, yes, I am luckier than I realized."

"Thank you." He said nothing more, merely leaning back in his chair with his eyes closed and his face relaxed.

A bit disappointed that he didn't have a greater reaction to her admission, Audrey began to read.

Nathan, however, picked up the pitcher and rose. "I'm going to return this to the icebox. I'd rather go for a walk." He started for the door, his steps firm and sure. Then he stopped, and the tips of his ears grew red. "That is, if you don't mind going for a walk."

"No, I—" Audrey's throat closed. She swallowed and tried again. "That sounds lovely. It's not in the least hot, and we can see if any of the leaves are turning color—ugh. I am sorry."

"It's all right, Audrey. I can see with my nose."

"I beg your pardon?"

Chuckling, he entered the house, sending the aroma of cooking apples and cinnamon billowing into the afternoon.

Audrey rolled her eyes and followed him. Inside the house, Sally and her mother clattered about in the kitchen, talking, laughing, and making enough noise for ten women. Or maybe all females in kitchens sounded like that. Audrey knew precious little about the work of canning and preserving. She supposed she should go in and learn from them, but she much preferred the world of books and medicine, dialogue and science.

Listening to the women try to foist help onto Nathan and his polite refusal, she returned the book to its shelf. She wasn't certain she could read *The Adventures of Huckleberry Finn* aloud. Some parts of it were pretty vulgar. Yet how could she deny him? He wanted to read the book, hadn't had the time while working in the city, then couldn't read it for himself. Who was she to judge what he should hear if she didn't want him telling her what medicine she could practice? He had assured her he wouldn't stop her from seeing patients who specifically requested her. She shouldn't dictate what he should read just because she disapproved.

Hearing him coming back, she tugged down the front of her dress to smooth out the creases. She would have to start wearing her widow's weeds again if she didn't get some new clothes made. She couldn't go around looking frumpy. Even if her husband couldn't see her, he deserved a well-groomed wife.

She raised her wrist to her nose and sniffed for her perfume. The dab of lilies-of-the-valley scent she'd placed there earlier had worn off. She should take the time to go upstairs to her room and sprinkle on more so he could find her with ease.

She'd left it until too late. He appeared in the parlor doorway and headed for the door. At the last moment he swerved to the side and stopped beside her.

"You came inside. Don't you want to go?"

"I brought the book in." She sniffed her other wrist. "How did you know I'm here? I can't smell my perfume anymore."

He laughed. "Audrey, I could find you in the middle of a field of lilies." He rested his hands on her shoulders and took a step closer to her. "Don't you understand that?" His voice dropped.

So did her stomach. No, that was her heart careening, tumbling, falling with dizzying haste. She didn't recognize the sensation of joy, fear, and anticipation colliding.

"I'm learning." She sounded breathless. Ridiculous.

"One thing at a time." His hands tightened their hold.

"Mrs. Maxwell?" Sally entered the parlor, wiping her hands on her apron. "Do you want that chicken fried or roasted for tonight?"

Too warm for the temperature of the house, Audrey turned away from Nathan to address Sally's question. Once the dinner was settled, she grasped Nathan's hand and all but dragged him outside.

"She should knock before walking into a room," Audrey groused as they headed down the drive. "My mother would dismiss a maid for just walking in and talking like that. I know Sally isn't really a servant, but there is common courtesy and— Why are you laughing at me?"

"I think you know." Nathan curved his hand around her arm. "Slow down. There's no fire."

"I'm sorry." Audrey slowed as they reached the road, crossed it, and entered a tract of wooded land with trees so high, they formed a cathedral ceiling with their overarching branches. "I don't know what got into me."

But she did. She was quite, quite certain Nathan had been about to kiss her when Sally interrupted him.

In three weeks of marriage he hadn't kissed her except for a light peck on the cheek. Today she was certain that had been about to change.

Not that she should care, for goodness sake. This was a marriage of convenience, not a love match. They had wedded out of a mutual need for companionship and support, nothing more.

Except for liking. Yes, they liked each other a great deal. Audrey liked him even more since that morning when he assured her he would not stop her from practicing and would not keep her fees as he had a right to do.

To add to his kindness, as they meandered through the woods seeking the glint of red or gold amidst the mostly green leaves and smelling the spiciness of drying foliage, Nathan offered her an allowance. "You won't always get paid promptly or at all by your patients, and you'll need to replenish your supplies. Then, of course, you'll need things for yourself. I've been a beast not to think of that before Corinne pinned back my ears about it. She'll pin yours back, too, for not asking."

"You've given me a home and protection for my baby. Why would I ask for more?"

Of course, he would get money from Doc that was rightfully hers—or maybe he wouldn't. A hint of resentment rose. She tamped it down. Arranged or not, her marriage was of her own choosing, and she had to accept the consequences of that. He was doing his best to make up for the drawbacks.

"And you've given me a great deal more. I—" He cleared his throat. "It's settled then. You should go into Winchester for anything you need, like ladies' things. Marysville doesn't have enough to offer if you prefer ready-made."

"I do." Audrey glanced at him, but his face revealed nothing of what he'd been about to say and decided against uttering. "I don't think I have time to sew things for myself."

At least she hoped she wouldn't have time. Unfortunately she'd had more than enough time not only to travel into Winchester and find ready-made garments that fit her expanding figure, but also to purchase fabric and make her own ball gown if she wished. She could have taken the train to Connecticut and placated her livid mother and former mother-in-law with the news of her hasty marriage to a near stranger.

She had no patients. As though the judge's decision to let Dr. Hornsby keep his practice banished from people's minds the memory of his overindulgence in spirits and consequent poor judgment as a physician, patients returned to him. Expectant women still used the midwife or even trusted Doc with their precious burdens.

"You're newly wed," a middle-aged neighbor had said on a call. "No one wants to disturb you. And there is your own . . . ahem . . ." Her gaze flicked to Audrey's middle.

"I'm perfectly capable," she protested to Nathan later that afternoon as they sat in the parlor.

"Yes, but you should see a doctor or the midwife yourself."

"I'll find a doctor in Winchester. I won't go to anyone in this county. I haven't heard much good of the midwife and wouldn't go near Dr. Hornsby." After a pause she dared add, "I wouldn't be surprised if he is spreading rumors about me to keep people away."

Nathan said nothing.

Her suspicion sharpened, Audrey glared at him. Realizing this would have no effect, she demanded, "What have you heard?"

He shrugged. "Nothing of any significance."

"Nathan."

"Only that you misdiagnosed Jasper Smithfield's broken toe as gout."

"I most certainly did not. You know I didn't. You were there. You—"

"Calm yourself, Audrey." Nathan patted her hand, but the twitching corners of his mouth didn't help to unruffle her. "I tried to counter the talk, but there was the hotel room incident and . . . Audrey, you're a stranger here. People here don't take to strangers very well."

"But . . . but everyone's been very kind." Audrey sagged against the back of her chair, her head spinning. "If they don't like me, why be so kind?"

They'd been inundated with callers, some who stayed for a minute, others who stayed so long, she wondered if they expected dinner and a bed for the night. All of them brought something along, from a jar of pickled watermelon rind, which she discovered she loved, to whole turkeys already dressed for roasting.

"Of course they're kind." Nathan's tone held a note of wonder, as though he couldn't believe she was so naive. "You're my wife."

"Are you saying—?" Audrey closed her eyes and took a few deep breaths. "Are you saying that if Adam and I had moved here on our own or if Dr. Hornsby had given me the practice without a fuss, we wouldn't have been as accepted?"

"You would have done all right." Nathan looked pensive.

"Folks need a doctor who isn't ten miles away or more. But, no, they wouldn't have welcomed you with quite so much enthusiasm."

"But that enthusiasm won't extend to people wanting me for their doctor if Dr. Hornsby is available."

"Of course some will. Look at Mrs. Wilson."

"Yes, Mrs. Wilson." Audrey pressed her cheek into a wing of the chair back. "You knew this would happen, didn't you?"

"I thought it might. People . . ." He rose, walked to a bookcase, and ran his hand over the spines as though in search of a volume. "Although I grew up here, I've had few visitors for the past two years. I'd become a stranger to them."

Her heart twisted. "I'm sorry, Nathan. I truly am. But I wish you'd warned me."

"And have you get on a train for Connecticut?"

There it was again, that tumbling, twisting sensation inside her.

"It'll be better now that everyone's met you." Nathan spoke a little faster than usual. "They realize you are polite and well spoken and will be of great use when it comes to needing extra hands for the county fair or church bazaar. You might not be able to cook, but you can sew. You're of use to them, so they'll accept you, and once they do that, they'll lo—like you. That's inevitable."

It wasn't the same with the men for him. Nathan, Audrey understood, didn't feel useful. No matter how much she tried to let him do as much as he could and kept her mouth shut about his carving, she knew he cringed when she was the one patching up the cuts and bruises that were common among workers on a farm during harvest.

Whatever else he wasn't saying hung in the air between them any time the conversation turned personal—he loved her.

Part of her wished he would admit it so she would have to respond and explore her feelings toward him. As matters stood, she pushed aside the odd effect being near him had on her heart, brain, and everything else. She didn't know if it was love. Love had eluded her in her first marriage, though she had tried to summon it. With Nathan she feared she only experienced a profound sense of gratitude mixed with respect and liking. She really hoped it wasn't pity. The only thing about Nathan to be pitied was the unfortunate circumstance of not being able to practice medicine.

If only there were a way . . .

The thought perturbed her so much, she spent hours combing through every medical text the two of them owned and the journals—American and English—that arrived in the mail. Her best idea seemed to be for him to teach. For that, however, she needed to persuade him to leave the Valley. And he wouldn't do that because it meant leaving his family and others who depended on him, like Doc.

Deciding to take up the matter with Corinne, Audrey prepared for the dinner with care. Her wardrobe was limited, but at least the golden-brown suit with the flaring skirt and stand-up collar looked autumnal and went well with her dark hair and eyes.

Nathan appeared to advantage in dark blue, which brought out the golden highlights in his hair, and she told him so.

"I'll return the compliment"—he grinned at her—"if you'll accept it."

"I will, thank you." She patted the carriage seat beside her. "Don't sit over there. I promise I don't bite."

"It's a small carriage. I wasn't sure there was room."

"Of course there is, for you."

They sat close and somehow ended up holding hands while exchanging light banter until they reached Corinne and Russell Chapman's house.

Until they heard the screams.

Chapter Twelve

By the time the second cry pierced the air between the house and the carriage, Nathan had pushed open the carriage door, leaped to the ground, and rushed toward the front door before he remembered he couldn't see where he was going and could trip and fall at any second. He stopped, a tremor racing through him as he struggled between taking the risk of injury and covering his ears to blot out the sound of his sister in labor.

His sister—in labor a month early.

His sister was in labor and, by the sound of it, having a bad time. Two years ago he could have helped. Two years ago he would already be at her side, assisting the doctor or midwife though doing nothing more, as doctors weren't supposed to work on family members. Corinne would be mortified to have him do so anyway, but in an emergency . . .

Another scream confirmed this was indeed an emergency.

Nathan pressed his fingertips to his temples and the twin scars, the symbols of his inability to help anyone now. For ten years he'd served those who could afford to pay him and those who couldn't. In a city full of wealthy and poor, he relieved what suffering he could. His reward was to have a thug hold a small-caliber pistol to his head and pull the trigger. And because of that he now couldn't help his sister and had possibly made matters worse for Audrey.

Not since the first days of waking to realize he lived, but without his sight, had Nathan felt so helpless and desperate for something to change. Regardless of the sorts of hazards always present when three small boys strew their toys around at random, he plunged forward. He must at least make certain Corinne had medical help of some sort.

"Wait." A velvety voice touched his ears as a gentle hand touched his arm. "There's a toy bat in front of you. If you step on it, you'll likely go flying into the boxwoods."

"Audrey." He gripped her hand. "Something's wrong. I wasn't here for Corinne's other deliveries, but Russ said they were easy. He actually stayed with her throughout the entire ordeal."

"What an exceptional husband." She started forward, something clattering over the gravel path ahead of them as though kicked out of the way. "I look forward to meeting him. Though I wish—" He felt her flinch at yet one more cry. "I wish these were better circumstances."

"Yes. Yes, I do too." He felt breathless, his heart pounding out of control. "I suppose I can keep him company. And the children. You can—"

They reached the front steps just as the door burst open. "Nathan, thank goodness you're here." Russell Chapman grasped Nathan's hand between his big, calloused palms. "The midwife . . . She's just sent for Doc, but my Corinne is in terrible trouble. I don't know what. The midwife doesn't know what. Man, you've got to do something."

Russell's voice was shaking. His hands were shaking.

"Russ, I can't do anything now." Each word tore from Nathan like stitches from a new wound. "But if Doc's coming, things—"

Yet one more shriek reverberated through the house and out the open door.

"I'm not certain there's time to wait for him." Audrey spoke with decisiveness. "Mr. Chapman, I am Dr. Audrey Van— Maxwell. I'm fully qualified to assist."

Except she wasn't supposed to once Doc was called.

But who cared about a judge's orders when Corinne was in desperate straits?

"May I go up?" Audrey asked.

"I-I suppose you can." Russell took a deep breath. "If you think it's all right, Nathan."

"She's fully qualified." Nathan's gut tightened, and he released Audrey's arm. "Maybe you can at least see what's wrong."

"We can see what's wrong." Audrey returned his hand to her arm. "You're coming with me."

"Audrey, I—"

She tugged him forward and over the threshold. "You have more experience with childbirth in your little finger than I have in my entire brain."

He held back. "Not anymore."

"Why not?" she demanded. "Why not?" Audrey stopped, swung to face him, and clamped her hands on his shoulders. "In the six weeks I've known you, I've come to understand that all that bullet did was rob you of your sight, not your brain. Your knowledge and experience are still there."

"But without seeing anything . . ."

Once again, he stood torn between a desire to dash up the steps to Corinne's side and race out the door to the safety of his own home and memories of when he had been sought after and purposeful.

"I'll be your eyes." She caressed his cheek. "Perhaps she won't need us at all. She might simply be suffering a bit more this time, and nothing is truly wrong."

"But the midwife thinks—" Russell sounded like he was about to weep. "She thinks it's a breech, and she can't turn it."

"We'll do what we can until Doc gets here." Nathan hoped his smile showed more confidence than he felt. "Why don't you . . . um . . ."

"Go to the children," Audrey suggested. "Where are they?"

"Out of earshot in the barn with some kittens." Russell gulped. "I'll make sure they're all right."

"You do that," Nathan and Audrey said together.

"No, wait," Audrey called out. "Go to our house and fetch my medical bag. Just in case I need it."

"But if something happens . . ." Russell protested.

"If something happens," Audrey persisted, "I'll need that bag."

"Go." Nathan spoke over another cry from Corinne that seemed weaker than its predecessors.

Not a good sign.

"Here's the banister." Audrey placed Nathan's hand on the smooth, polished wood. "I'll go ahead of you."

She took the steps faster than he thought a lady in her condition should be able to. He dogged her heels every step of the way, around the turn at the landing, and up another flight to the source of the distressed cries and the sound of a woman weeping.

This woman met them at the top of the stairs. "Oh, you're not the doctor. Mercy, mercy, I'm right sure she's going to die."

"She's a doctor," Nathan said.

"We're both doctors." Audrey spoke with emphasis.

"But you're a female, and he can't see," the woman wailed. "Oh, where is Doc?"

"She is a fully qualified doctor." Nathan gripped the newel post at the top of the railing. "And I . . . I know a great deal about childbirth. Are you the midwife?""

"I am, and I haven't lost a child or mother in fifteen years. Now I'm so sure—oh!" Her speech ended in a yelp when another scream from Corinne was heard.

"Go downstairs and wait for Dr. Hornsby." Nathan injected into his tone all the command he remembered from his days of practice. "He could take hours to get here."

"And we don't have hours," Audrey added.

She grabbed his hand and led him into a room near the head of the stairs. Corinne's room.

"Nathan . . . Audrey." Corinne greeted them in gasps. "This is . . . bad."

"Either that or you're just a rank coward." Nathan forced himself to smile as he reached his sister's bedside and stretched his hand toward her.

She clasped his hand, her grasp weaker than he wished it to be. "Don't let my baby die, Nathan."

"We won't let you or the baby die." Nathan hoped he said nothing but the truth. "Audrey worked at the New York Infirmary for a year."

"Mrs. Blair has been a midwife for thirty years," Corinne murmured. "She's very—" She broke off with another cry. Her hand gripped Nathan's so hard, he felt the bones grind together.

"Audrey?" He failed to suppress the edge of panic in his tone.

"May I examine you, Corinne?" Audrey asked, sounding calm.

He'd always managed that tone in the worst of circumstances. But now he employed every bit of control to stop himself from shaking. If only he weren't helpless and useless.

No, not useless. He was a supportive presence for Corinne and Audrey. But standing still made him want to yell with frustration.

"Do . . . what you must," Corinne whispered.

"I'll just leave the sheet draped over you to preserve your modesty," Audrey began in her velvety, soothing voice.

She kept up the patter, never changing her pitch, never stopping even when Corinne cried out.

"There, that wasn't so bad, was it?" Audrey touched Nathan's arm. "We're going to step out for just a minute. Rest all you can. It's going to be a long night."

Heart pounding, Nathan followed Audrey into the corridor. She pulled the door shut, and he thought she leaned against it.

"It is breech," she said. "And the reason she can't turn it even with her wonderfully small hands is because it's twins."

"Oh, dear—" Nathan pressed his hands to his temples.

Not so long ago, a pronouncement like that meant nearly certain death for the mother. Now, however, one way existed that could save her.

"If only I—maybe Doc will get here soon."

Hooves clattered on the drive.

"If that's him," Audrey said, "it's soon enough. If it's not . . . Nathan, I'm going to have to perform the procedure within the next thirty minutes."

"You can't."

"Why not? Do you think the judge is going to throw me in prison for performing an emergency caesarian on a woman to save her life?"

"If Doc's angry enough about it, he might."

"If either of them are, then they don't deserve the positions of trust they hold. And I'm willing to take the risk to save your sister's life."

Nathan took a deep breath as the front door slammed and Russell called up to them. "The risk may lie in letting you go ahead with your inexperience instead of waiting for Doc."

"We can wait a few minutes. But, Nathan—" She clutched both of his hands in hers. "I'm not without experience. But what's more important is that I have you with me."

"How can I possibly help?"

"You can talk me through it. You can observe her vital signs and administer the ether."

"You trust me with that? Audrey, I could miscalculate."

"Anyone could miscalculate. I really don't think we should wait."

"What news?" Russell shouted up to them.

"She's getting weaker," Audrey whispered.

"Do you have that bag?" Nathan called down to his brother-in-law. "We're going to need it."

Dr. Hornsby arrived just as Audrey was bandaging Corinne's belly and the midwife was tucking Corinne's second daughter, washed, dried, and warmly wrapped, into the cradle beside her sister. Both girls were tiny, perfectly formed, and breathing gently in their warm nest beside the fire. Their mother breathed a bit more heavily, still sleeping off the effects of the ether.

Coming up the steps, Dr. Hornsby sounded like a locomotive huffing and puffing steam on its way to a station. Audrey smelled no spirits on that breath, only a blend of garlic and onions and mint attempting to mask the former odors. But the blaze in his eyes warned her the next few minutes were going to be unpleasant.

"What have you done?" His voice was low, much like the growl of a large feline about to spring on its territorial enemy. "There's blood everywhere. Did you kill her?"

"She saved her life, Doc." Nathan spoke from his position at the head of the bed. "If she hadn't surgically removed the children—"

"Surgically removed—" Dr. Hornsby's eyes bulged.

Despite herself, Audrey flinched. She kept her mouth shut and continued to minister to her patient.

"Madam, you had no business touching my patient, let alone performing a dangerous operation." Dr. Hornsby grabbed her arm. "I'll have you jailed. I'll have you—"

"What's all the ruckus?" Corinne's sleepy voice broke into Doc's tirade.

Audrey yanked her arm free of his grasp and hastened to Corinne's side. "Good. You're coming out of the anesthesia. Are you in pain?"

Stupid question. Corinne must be in agony.

"My babies." Corinne tried to sit up. "Where are my babies?"

"Shh." Nathan rested his hand on her shoulder, holding her down. "You have two beautiful daughters. But you need to rest."

"Rest?" Dr. Hornsby loomed up on Corinne's other side. "You're lucky you're not dead, allowing that quack—"

"I am a fully qualified doctor." Audrey felt like a parrot with only one line whenever she was around Dr. William Hornsby.

"No fully qualified doctor—"

"Loses a mother and two babies because she's afraid to take a risk." Nathan spoke with quiet firmness while smoothing hair away from Corinne's brow. "We'll get you something for the pain."

Prompted to focus on her patient, Audrey hastened to mix a few drops of laudanum in a glass of water and take it to Corinne.

"What are you giving her?" Doc snatched the glass from Audrey's hand, spilling some its contents on the coverlet.

"It's laudanum." Audrey glared at him. "I suppose you prefer—"

Nathan clamped his hand on her wrist, a silent warning to say no more.

"If you would prefer to administer the draft, the bottle is on the table there." She smiled and left the room before her knees gave way or she was sick, or both.

She staggered down the steps and sought refuge in the empty parlor. Soon, someone would have to go out to the barn to inform Russell and the boys that they had two girls in their midst. Russ would want to see Corinne and assure himself she was all right before the mild opiate took complete effect.

And she was all right, thanks to Nathan's verbal guidance

and Audrey's determination not to give in to her fear. Nothing had gone wrong, and if she could keep infection away . . .

But what was she thinking? She had no control over Corinne now. She had sent for Dr. Hornsby, not her sister-in-law. Corinne was Doc's patient, not Audrey's. Audrey wasn't supposed to poach patients.

Surely the judge would understand that the life of the mother had been at stake and they couldn't risk waiting for Doc. But the man was so angry, Audrey wouldn't be surprised if he retaliated in whatever way he could, such as claiming Audrey had acted in haste to glorify herself.

As if any doctor would willingly cut into flesh to gain glory.

But she was just tired, shaking, and ill from having performed her second caesarian with the help of a panicked midwife and a former doctor who could no longer see. So much could have gone wrong.

She didn't realize she was crying until a hand touched her shoulder, then strong arms closed around her, drawing her against a broad shoulder.

"It's all right," Nathan murmured, stroking her hair. "You did everything just fine."

"I could have killed her." Audrey gulped down a sob. "I could have killed the babies."

"Not having done it could have just as easily killed all of them." He raised one hand to her face and brushed away her tears. "But it didn't."

She raised her head and managed a wobbly smile. "I couldn't have done it without you."

"I wasn't of much use." The joy on his face belied his words. "You could have managed without me."

"No, I don't believe I could have." She cupped her hands around his jaw. "I-I needed you there."

"I like to think you need me more than there." His smile was rueful.

Audrey backed away from the jolt of joy spiking through her at his words. "Dr. Hornsby will give us trouble. He seems unreasonably angry."

"Unfortunately but not unreasonably." Nathan sighed. "Since you did that surgery successfully on Mrs. Wilson, he's felt threatened by you. To have a female preferred to him hit him hard at a time when he was just getting back on his feet. It's fear talking, my—Audrey. It's fear his skill really has slipped over these past two years and of you with your fancy European education."

"But I'm not a threat. People here want to support him, the local man. You said it yourself. I'm the outsider."

"You won't be after this." He twined a strand of her tumbled hair around his finger. "You took a risk to save someone special to most everyone around."

"It's a risk I took for you, because of you, with you." She let out a shaky laugh. "I don't know what I'm saying except . . . Except—" Her mouth went dry, and the words caught in her throat, words she didn't dare let loose for fear she was wrong, merely overwrought, and swooning with gratitude.

But then he kissed her, and her heart cried out so loudly, she thought perhaps he heard, for he was the one to say them aloud.

"I love you."

No, no, no, she knew she should cry out in response. She didn't really love him; she was only grateful for what he had done for her, for giving her the freedom to practice her profession without the risk of losing control over her child. Likewise, he only loved her for letting him help her and practice his profession even in a small way. Gratitude was not love.

But this certainly felt different from her feelings for Adam.

She dropped her head against his chest, listening to the steady beat of his heart, and ached to have the true freedom of being able to tell him she loved him too.

She didn't know how long they stood there, close, silently

communicating and relieved that all had gone so well for Corinne and the babies. A discreet cough from the doorway made them jump apart like two adolescents caught misbehaving.

"Is . . . everything all right?" Russell's hesitance in asking demonstrated the anxiety apparent in his twisting hands and ashen face.

"Everything is under control." Nathan headed for his brother-in-law, hand extended. "Congratulations. You are the father of two perfect little girls."

"Girls?" Russ' face lit. "And Corinne?"

"She will be all right." Nathan glanced back at Audrey and smiled. "Thanks to my wife."

"What do you mean, 'will be'?" Russell clasped Nathan's hand, more like a drowning man clutching a lifeline, not the handshake of friendship. "What happened?"

"It was necessary—"

Feet thudding on the steps broke into Nathan's explanation.

"To perform surgery to deliver the babies."

"Tell him the truth, Maxwell." Dr. Hornsby leaned over the stair railing so his face appeared in the parlor doorway above Russ'. "She risked your wife's life, and it could still be at risk if the incision grows septic."

"It was necessary," Audrey protested, noting that Nathan had spoken exactly the same words.

"How do you know it was necessary, Maxwell?" Hornsby demanded, ignoring her. "Did you examine the mother?"

"No, but—" Nathan's face turned stony. "I trusted Audrey's description as I would any colleague's."

"That's peculiar." Doc's upper lip curled. "Considering you said something quite different to the judge not a month ago."

Chapter Thirteen

Audrey walked home from the Chapmans'. She was so exhausted, she could barely put one foot in front of the other, but she traversed the two miles in the chilly October night with a nearly full moon glowing as orange as a pumpkin overhead and a few lingering crickets serenading her. Once in the farmhouse she went to her room and locked the door behind her.

She supposed the thing to do was to fling herself across the bed and weep over her husband's betrayal. Instead, she undressed with care, washed in the dressing room that had been turned into a bathroom, slid between lavender-scented sheets, and willed herself to sleep. She would think in the morning. Everything looked brighter in the light of day and after a good night's sleep. In the morning she wouldn't feel as though Doc's words had ripped her heart from its moorings.

Vaguely, she recalled Nathan knocking on her door and asking if she was all right. She assured him she was and returned to sleep.

"Morning," she murmured to herself. "Joy comes in the morning."

Except in the morning, she felt worse. Her heart ached, and the nausea that had left her weeks earlier returned with a vengeance.

Perhaps everyone was right, she thought, as she wiped cold perspiration from her brow. She should give up notions of practicing medicine and concentrate on being a mother. Every upset seemed to make the baby squirm and her stomach rebel.

Yet she'd promised Adam she would keep up her profession. She'd given him so little in life, the least she could do was to keep her promise to him in death. For a second time she'd married without love to keep her promise to Adam.

Except the marriage wasn't without love now, and the man who had finally won her heart had done his best to ensure she would not keep a deathbed promise to her first husband.

"How could I be so stupid?" She covered her face with her hands and wished the pain weren't too deep for tears. "I should have gone home."

At least then she wouldn't be permanently tied to a man who had misled her if not outright lied to her. At least then she wouldn't have alienated her mother and former mother-in-law.

But she still would have found keeping her promise to Adam difficult.

"But not impossible." Her hands balled into fists she pounded against her thighs.

Nor was it impossible now.

For weeks she had accepted the fact that she had no patients. She hadn't liked it, but she had done nothing to overcome the problem either. Now, with the memory of safely delivering Corinne of two babies, however drastic the measures taken, fresh in her mind, Audrey doubted she could sit back and wait for the sick and injured to come to her.

Plans whirling through her head, she buttoned her jacket over a middle that was expanding farther than she thought proper for a lady wishing to go out and heal the sick and injured, and descended the steps. The smell of coffee and bacon drew her to the kitchen. After her earlier bout of nausea, she was now starving.

Until she came face-to-face with Nathan sitting in the breakfast room. Morning sunlight kissed the gold highlights in his hair and bronzed his features, so that his blue eyes shone with the rich blue found in imported porcelain.

How fortunate for him that the gunshot that blinded him hadn't taken his eyes. Fortunate for everyone who enjoyed the pleasure of seeing their gorgeous color.

Or unfortunate, perhaps, for Audrey, who felt as weak-kneed as a schoolgirl with her first penchant for the opposite sex.

Her only true penchant for the opposite sex. In school, she had found her studies far more interesting than the young men who came around to court the young ladies.

Then Nathan Maxwell walked into her life, and she nearly forgot her passion for medicine.

Her feelings for him and her feelings toward her profession collided there in the doorway to the breakfast room. The conflicting emotions grabbed at her middle, twisting her stomach into a knot and reducing her tongue to a useless lump in her mouth.

Nathan turned his face toward her and gave her a half smile. "I waited to eat like one pig waits for another." He indicated his nearly empty plate. "But I think something's left. A crumb or two."

"That's enough." Audrey selected a piece of toast, dabbed it with a spoonful of strawberry preserves, and poured herself a cup of coffee.

"You should have some applesauce too," Nathan said.

She started to ask him how he could possibly know she wasn't eating any, then realized he would have heard her spooning the cooked fruit into a bowl.

"All right." She took a small amount.

"More."

"Are you trying to fatten me up?"

"I'm trying to keep you healthy. You didn't eat supper last night."

"So I didn't." She filled the bowl and slid a slice of bacon onto her plate. "I forgot."

No wonder she hadn't felt well that morning.

She headed for the table.

Nathan jumped up and drew out a chair.

The one next to his.

Well, so he wanted it out or to be friendly enough for her to forget it. It. His betrayal.

She smacked her plate and cup onto the table with more force than necessary. "Have your say."

"Audrey." He turned to her and curved his fingers around her arm, urging her to sit. "Don't ever do that again."

"Don't ever do what again? Save your sister's life, not to mention your nieces'?"

"That's not what I'm talking about, and you know it." A muscle jumped on the side of his jaw. "Don't ever walk off into the dark like that. There are still dangerous animals around, and not all of them have four legs."

"I was perfectly all right." She bowed her head, fighting tears. "I couldn't stay. I wasn't wanted."

"I wanted you there."

Her heart leaped. She squashed it into place.

"Did you, when you had to choose between your old friend and your new wife?"

"I—" Sighing, he removed his hand from her arm and rubbed his temples. "I never wanted to be caught between Doc and you."

"But you were." She made her voice as steely as she could manage. "And you chose him."

"Audrey—"

"What exactly did you tell the judge?"

"You were there. You know I told him nothing directly." He shoved his plate toward the center of the table and gripped the edge with both hands. "That is, I didn't say anything to him in the official context of your contract hearing. I've known him all my life, so when I was in town and we had coffee together at the hotel, I commented on how well Doc was doing since you came into town. How well I was doing too." He flashed her a tentative smile. "And how I worried about Doc if he were to lose his practice altogether. I didn't think he would be so harsh with you."

"But you must have known that what you said would influence the judge to side with Dr. Hornsby." Audrey barely managed to get the words past her stiff lips.

Color tinged Nathan chiseled cheekbones. "I only hoped it would influence him to let Doc keep the practice if he paid you back the money."

"I suppose I should be grateful to you for being honest to me . . . now." Audrey rose, shoving her chair back so hard, it hit the wall. "A pity you weren't when I agreed to marry you."

"Of course I was honest with you then too." Nathan stood, much taller and broader than she was, blocking her way unless she skirted the table.

She considered doing just that for a moment, but the grief on Nathan's face stopped her. Just because he'd taken her heart and crushed it didn't mean she should do the same to him.

Not that he knew her heart was his. She had stopped herself from admitting it the night before. Perhaps she could take it back and forget she cared so much that she wanted to rest her head on his shoulder and say she didn't care if she never saw another patient in her life if that would make him happy.

The suspicion that her discontinuing practicing medicine would indeed make him happy, while making her miserable, kept her standing upright, stiff-spined, and resolved.

"I meant every word I said when I promised I wouldn't interfere with you and patients who came your way." Nathan looked anything but happy as he spoke to her. "Nor did I promise I would abandon my friend for the sake of your career. For as long as he's capable of practicing, I don't want him to stop."

"But you don't mind if I have to stop? It's all right if he spreads lies about me so I have no patients?"

"Of course not. Audrey, please understand that—"

"Understand what?" Her voice rose. She knew she should calm herself, not let Sally somewhere in the house overhear her, and not let her mouth get ahead of her brain, but her tongue felt like a runaway wagon zipping downhill—unstoppable. "That you can't practice anymore so you don't want me to either?"

She slapped her hand over her mouth far too late. Too late to hold the words in. Too late to prevent her accusation from making Nathan flinch so hard, she saw his body recoil, every muscle in his face tensing it into a frozen, expressionless mask.

"It's not true." He spoke as though from a long way off. "But all the denials in the world won't convince you otherwise, will they?"

Her throat closed, and she couldn't speak.

"I suppose if I let you appeal the judge's decision and take this to a trial, it might convince you." Slowly, Nathan pushed in his chair. "But if it doesn't, I've risked hurting my old friend for nothing. Now, if you will excuse me, I hear James outside, and I need to speak with him."

His steps even and firm, he headed for the back door.

Audrey didn't hear James outside. She didn't hear Sally inside. She could swear she heard her heart ripping in two.

And with the pain arrived anger and outrage that her husband had chosen to stand by his friend instead of her.

Well, if no one would stand by her, she would simply have

to fight for herself and her right to practice her profession. She'd allowed Adam and now Nathan to take care of her instead of taking care of herself. Allowing it hadn't been a mistake precisely; she had simply grown too used to relying on their help. She must now learn to rely on herself if the baby she carried would be depending on her in a few months.

Too few months.

December had seemed so far off in the heat of summer, but as she woke almost every morning to the sparkle of frost on the grass, she realized how swiftly the year was slipping behind her.

So was her brief but satisfying friendship with her husband. Since their encounter at breakfast and her tactless remark about his motives, they had carried on like polite strangers. She still read to him and took him for walks with her, but their dialogue was sparse and impersonal.

If only she felt impersonal toward him. Every time he took her arm for a stroll through the woods, she remembered his kissing her and telling her he loved her, and her heart twisted with longing. Every time he rode into town with James, she knew he was visiting Doc, and her muscles tensed with thoughts of how he chose friendship over love.

Yet hadn't she chosen profession over family?

The thought struck her one day as she penned a duty letter to the mothers. Neither of them had written to her. Her father had sent her a ten-dollar coin, as though she were a schoolgirl, and a brief note telling her to save it for an emergency. She had no idea what that emergency might be or why he thought she might need it. She tucked the gold piece into her handkerchief in the event something arose and went about thinking of ways to have patients ask for her.

If she called on Corinne . . .

She sent a note around to Corinne to ask if she minded

company. Audrey wasn't poaching on Doc's territory; she was calling on her sister-in-law.

Corinne responded within the hour. In handwriting so shaky it revealed she was still weak from her traumatic delivery, she requested that Audrey come immediately. Since Nathan was in town, Audrey complied.

Corinne half reclined in her bed, her face ashen yet radiant as she fed both of her daughters at once.

"Without all these pillows I'd never be able to hold them," she admitted. "But I'd never get any sleep if I took them one at a time."

"I'm pleased you can feed them at all." Audrey perched on the chair beside the bed and stroked one baby's silky cheek with a forefinger, though her arms ached to cradle one or both of the girls. "They're beautiful."

Blond fuzz covered their heads, and their eyes were as blue as their mother's.

As their uncle's.

"Russ is besotted." Corinne bowed her head over her babies. "I am too. After three boys, girls will be so much fun and trouble of a different kind."

"Have you named them?"

"Yes. Pearl and Opal. Our jewels." Corinne laughed and winced. "But I feel like you delivered them with a hacksaw." She peeked at Audrey from beneath her gold-tipped lashes. "To listen to Doc, you did."

Audrey straightened herself, chin jutting. "I made the smallest, neatest incision possible. But those are big girls for early twins."

"That's what Nathan said." Now Corinne fully looked at Audrey, a crease between her fine brows. "He's really wonderful with them, so gentle. I never thought about how many babies he handled in his practice, but he is experienced, and not being able to see what he's doing has nothing to do with his ability to cuddle them. I think they already adore him."

"I . . . I didn't realize he'd been here." Audrey rose and went to the hearth, where a fire burned to stave off the chill of the misty afternoon. "He went out but didn't say where."

"Where did you think he was? No, no, wait, will you come get these piglets before I drop them?"

"Of course." Audrey returned to the bed and took first one, then the other baby from their mother's arms. She noticed they needed to be changed, so she tended to that before laying them in their cradle. All the while, one of them cooed at her, and the other appeared to sleep, her mouth moving as though still nursing.

Their mother watched Audrey, her brows knitted again and her lips compressed in a thin line. To Audrey, Corinne appeared angry. Audrey could imagine why. She had come along, foisted herself into their family, and had the audacity—no, the heartlessness—to say something unforgivable to Nathan.

She shouldn't have come. In no way would Corinne be inclined to help her.

Audrey went to the door. "I should leave. Thank you for letting me see the girls. They appear to be thriving."

"But you haven't asked how I'm doing." Corinne spoke with an exaggerated whine.

Audrey clasped her hands over her expanding middle. "You're not my patient."

"No, I'm your sister-in-law—forever." Corinne's eyes narrowed. "Or are you thinking of leaving my brother?"

"No, never. We're married."

"From what I've read of Society, that doesn't seem to matter much anymore."

"It matters to me." Audrey returned to the chair, her knees weak, her throat tight. "I took a vow."

"And you're in love with him." Corinne reached out a hand to Audrey.

She took it and fixed her gaze on the cradle, where the girls slept side by side. "We were friends at least. Now we're polite strangers."

"You hurt him badly." Corinne's tone was matter-of-fact, not censorious.

Still, Audrey flinched. "He hurt me badly."

"Audrey, he spoke up for Doc without thinking of the consequences to you. The result wasn't intented."

"Oh, but it was." Audrey felt sick. "He's admitted as much to me. He said he hoped his words would influence the judge in Doc's favor."

"But you can't be sure the judge would have decided things differently."

"No, but the damage is done."

"Permanently?"

"I don't know." Audrey sighed. "Perhaps if I had patients and he had . . . something, we could rebuild our friendship, even if there's little hope of anything else building between us."

Through the window she caught the sound of children's excited laughter and a male timbre joining in. Russ and the boys were coming back from wherever they'd been. Audrey would have to go soon so as not to intrude on the family.

She slid to the edge of her chair.

"Wait." Corinne gripped Audrey's hand more tightly. "Why do you think there can be nothing more between you and my brother?"

"Nathan has made it clear he's chosen old friendships above a new wife." Audrey swallowed the bitter taste of rejection in her mouth. "And I-I'm not sure how much I can dare to love someone who has done that to me. I've already lost a husband because he put the pleasure of boating above his wife and child."

"Oh, you poor thing." Sympathy softened Corinne's features. "My heart aches for you. I want to help any way I can."

"Thank you, but I can't ask." Audrey hoped Corinne would read her mind.

A door slammed below stairs.

"We'll be swarmed in moments." Corinne grinned. "So I'll talk fast. Yes, I'm Doc's patient, but I know what you did for me, and once I tell everyone, you'll get patients aplenty, Jasper Smithfield's big toe or not. Yes, I think that's what I need to do—get you patients to serve as long as you're physically able to do so."

"But if Nathan still has nothing . . ." Audrey kept all hope from her voice.

"Nathan?" Corinne's smile tightened at the corners. "He's already got his own plans."

Chapter Fourteen

Nathan wandered around his den, running his fingers over the leather-bound volumes of his medical books and the paper spines of the journals. From there he moved to the polished surface of his desk, the silver inkwell, and the row of steel-nibbed pens that were no longer of any use to him. He crossed the room to lean against the backs of the two chairs in which he and Audrey had spent so many contented—no, happy—hours talking, reading, or sitting in companionable silence.

He liked to think he'd taught her how to appreciate the world by smell, touch, and sound. The autumn leaves were acrid but sweet-scented. Canada geese heading south grew distressed when separated from their flock and cried in a different tone. Autumn breezes on a bright day held a chill in the center and the warmth of the sun around the edges. To him, she described the colors of the sky. "Blue a shade paler than your eyes." The oak leaves. "The same brown as your hair but without the golden highlights." The walnuts strewing the ground. "The color of that velvet smoking jacket of yours, which is the silliest thing you own, since you don't smoke."

Every detail spoke of her affection for him. He'd even begun to hope it spoke of love. He certainly knew how much he loved her. If he hadn't fallen in love with her at first—well, sound of her mellow voice—he'd certainly tumbled head over heels for her the day she stitched up his hand. She'd been more than competent; she had exuded a caring he had only hoped to demonstrate to his patients and feared he'd never quite achieved.

She was an excellent doctor, and a few careless words, however well intended, had set her back in practicing a profession for which she obviously had skill, talent, and passion. All his hopes that she would never find out or that, if she did, things would be going so well for her that she wouldn't care died the instant Doc opened his mouth.

"I did you a favor out of loyalty." Nathan spoke his thoughts aloud. "And you ruined my marriage out of fear or jealousy or just plain spite."

Instead of confronting Doc about it, Nathan had gone to him and asked if he could work with him. "I've worked with Audrey twice now, talking her through her cases. I might not be able to do the actual work, but I have a great deal of knowledge."

Doc had responded with an uncommitted, "I'll think about it."

"You don't have to pay me. I just want something to do," Nathan had assured his mentor.

Nathan had hoped for a good outcome, but Doc's continued silence on the matter, and the way he avoided the subject whenever Nathan paid him a visit, was answer enough. Nor did Audrey request his company on her calls anymore.

And calls she had, for Doc hadn't ruined Audrey's medical practice, or, at least, the emergency surgery to deliver Corinne's twins had compensated for harmful talk about Audrey. Within two weeks of the twins' birth Audrey had been called out to at least one patient a day, sometimes two. She now boasted nearly twenty patients who had asked for her care instead of Doc's.

They were mostly uncomplicated matters like a child with a persistent cough or a woman suspecting she was in a delicate condition and wanting confirmation. Today, however, despite a cold November rain that threatened to turn to sleet at higher elevations, Audrey had gone up the mountain with a patient's frantic husband because, once again, the midwife suspected a breech birth.

"I should have gone with her." Nathan paced around his den again, then settled on one of the wing-backed chairs and picked up his carving.

It was almost finished and resembled a dog. The ears weren't set evenly on the head, one eye was a bit too big, and Nathan had lopped off its tail the day he cut his hand, yet it pleased him to have accomplished something. It was very smooth, and maybe Audrey would like it or her baby could use it for teething. The ebony had taken so much effort to cut, Nathan doubted tiny baby teeth could dent let alone splinter it. He would polish it further and give it to Audrey, if she wanted it.

She seemed to want only one thing from him these days. Nothing else, he feared, would repair his marriage.

Repair? Give it any hope of being happy and loving. Once he knew how to repair the matter for the good of all involved, he kept telling himself, he would have that conversation with Doc.

It hadn't been right for weeks. Listening to the rain patter against the windows behind him, Nathan accepted he would have to make the time right. The time for letting others come to him had passed. If he wanted to win the heart of the lady he loved, he needed to take the risk of putting himself forward, taking his sister's advice, and embellishing it further with his own plan.

The distant whicker of a horse from the stable drove home the fact that he couldn't leave for town that instant. Every time he gained resolve, no one was available to drive him, so he stewed, thought some more, and reconsidered his actions.

"Tomorrow." He spoke with resolve. "Rain or shine, I'll go."

Meanwhile he prepared to spend a long, lonely night by the fire. Sally was capable of seeing to the house and proved to be an excellent cook with the help of her mother, but she wasn't good company. Unlike Ruby, Sally was intimidated by him and wouldn't carry on even the most lighthearted of conversations with him.

Maybe Ruby could come home. The first frost had certainly been hard enough to kill off the foliage that seemed to bring on her coughing and wheezing spells. Doc was doing well enough now to be able to afford a housekeeper. That way, when Audrey was away, Ruby and James would keep him company.

They could even keep him company half of the time Audrey was home.

Hearing wheels on the drive, he smoothed his brow and rose to greet whoever had come. It was Audrey home early, he hoped. If she talked about her patient, he could feel like he was participating and perhaps even being useful in the aftermath of fear, worry, and excitement that usually followed an emergency.

He opened the front door in time to hear his wife thanking someone for the lift and the heartfelt, "You're welcome. Thank you," in response.

Her footfalls, still light and quick, crunched across the gravel, then resounded on the wooden steps of the porch. "Good evening, Nathan. I can see you've been carving again."

"How? Oh." Cheeks warming, he brushed shavings from the front of his coat.

"Here." She took his hand and tugged him into the parlor. "It's cold and wet out there, and you'll need a clothes brush to get that off. But at least I don't see any blood."

He thought he heard affection in her tone.

He raised his hand to her cheek and found it indeed cold

and damp. "Come into the den. There's a warm fire there. Are you hungry? Sally left your dinner on the stove."

"I am starving and rather tired." She headed for the den.

He squelched the urge to tell her she shouldn't be jaunting about the countryside in her condition.

"You're home earlier than I expected." He followed her into the warm room. "Was it a false alarm?"

"No, not at all. Oh, this fire feels wonderful. But we're low on wood. I'll go get—"

"Audrey, sit down. I can get more wood."

He didn't wait to find out if she listened to him. He veered toward the kitchen and back door and the wood stacked beneath the roof of the porch to keep it dry. He loaded his arms with fragrant logs, then made his way back through the house. Without a free hand to hold out in front of him, he veered off course twice, just enough to stub his foot on the leg of the piano no one played and his elbow on the frame of a door. Though he gritted his teeth, a gasp escaped from his lips.

"Are you all right?" Her heels struck the floor as she jumped to her feet. "Let me—"

"Audrey, please sit down. I'm not one of your patients," he snapped. "I'm your husband, and I'm capable of carrying in an armful of wood."

"Yes, but—"

"If I hurt myself, you can patch me up." He found the wood box with his foot and lowered the logs into the container. "Right now you need to rest and warm yourself. I'll get your dinner."

Once again he left her with as much speed as he could manage without hurting himself or breaking something. He only singed his fingers a bit retrieving the plate Sally had left warming on the stove. He found a tray, poured her a glass of milk, and carried the lot back to the den. He suspected the milk sloshed over the rim of the glass a bit, and he heard the silverware slide together on the tray instead of remaining neatly aligned, but she made no complaint, thanked him, and praised the venison stew and fresh cornbread.

"I never realized the weather could be so different on the mountain." She spoke between bites. "When we left, it was beginning to sleet, and some of the puddles were iced over. But it's only cold down here. Cold and muddy. I thought I'd never get warm again, but this fire feels wonderful."

"And how was your patient? Did everything go all right?"

"In the end, yes. When did you eat?"

"An hour ago. Audrey, I don't care about the weather or food. I care about what happened today."

"It ended up being quite routine." He heard indifference in her tone.

It made him feel like he'd banged his heart into a door frame.

"Will you please tell me about it?" He leaned toward her, hoping to convince her of his interest.

Her fork clattered against her plate. "Nathan, if you don't want me practicing medicine, you surely don't want to hear about my cases."

"You're wrong on both counts. I do want you practicing medicine. Why do you think I married you?"

He bit down on his tongue, realizing that wasn't quite the truth, but it was too late. The words were said.

"You showed your interest in my practicing my profession in a peculiar way." Dishes rattled. Her chair creaked. "If you'll excuse me, I would like to get my notes written up, then go to bed."

"I'd like you to stay."

She didn't. He could have followed her. But he did enough following people around to keep from foisting himself off on his wife like that. Instead, while he heard her in the kitchen washing up her dishes, he took the carving of the dog and carried it upstairs.

After only a little hunting around and much inhaling of her delicious fragrance, he found the stand beside her bed and set the carving on top. He managed to reach his own room across the hall just as she started up the steps. Leaning against his closed door, he listened.

After what seemed like an hour but must have been less than a quarter hour, since he heard no clock chime, he caught the sound of a soft laugh, then the quick patter of her footfalls in the hall.

"Nathan?" she called outside his door.

He opened it, probably too soon. "Yes?"

"Yes, indeed, you sneak." She touched his hand. "Thank you. It's delightful."

"It's not very good." He caught hold of her fingers and clasped them. "I'm sure those Parisian artists did much better."

"They had two good eyes, and yet . . ." She cleared her throat. "But I really wish you wouldn't risk hurting yourself again with sharp tools."

"And I wish you wouldn't travel into the mountains when the weather's bad, but I'm not going to stop you."

"I'm not going to stop you, of course. It's just that I worry."

"So do I." He smiled at her.

She gave a tentative chuckle. "I guess we're even."

"Not quite, but it's a start."

He wanted to hold her, but having his fingers laced with hers was a good start.

She tightened their hold. "I-I suppose if you truly do want to hear about what happened today, I can tell you."

"Can you make hot chocolate?"

This was one domestic skill she had acquired in Paris. She made them chocolate, and they returned to the den and the fire, and maybe the beginning of a new companionship or the rebuilding of their earlier friendship.

He could always hope.

"I was almost too late," she explained, sipping the rich dark chocolate. "We made good time getting there, but she made us wait for half an hour before she let me see her."

"Why?" Nathan posed the question, though he guessed the answer.

He'd encountered such scenarios before.

"She didn't think she was decent enough for a stranger to see her. The woman had to be in terrible pain, but she insisted the midwife comb her hair and help her put on a shirtwaist and jacket. Then she wouldn't let me look beneath the bedclothes. I had to do everything by touch."

"I approve of modesty in women when it's appropriate." Nathan nodded in understanding. "But most females take it too far."

"I don't know what I would have done if she had needed a caesarian."

"She didn't?"

"No, by the time I got to examine her, the baby was turning himself. I gave him a little help, and all went well."

"So you could come home to me." Nathan stretched his legs toward the hearth and cradled his cup in his hands, feeling warmth stealing through his whole body. "Was this her first?"

"Her fifth. The midwife said she's always like that."

As naturally as they had in the beginning, they slipped into medical talk and touched on a few memories of training before they began to yawn. The fire had died down, so they decided they might as well go to their rooms.

In the morning, more hopeful, more determined, Nathan opened his bedroom door, expecting to hear Audrey's voice amidst the female chatter downstairs. Instead, he heard Ruby bossing Sally around.

"Well, I'm here now. You get home to that man of yours. He's gonna need a lot of care and lovin' to keep him from gettin' cranky."

Concerned over this last remark, Nathan charged down the steps. "What happened?"

"Louis broke his leg this morning." Sally sniffled. "He fell out of the hayloft."

"Is Dr. Maxwell with him?" Nathan asked.

"Yes, sir. I came and got her right away." Sally gulped. "And I stayed to get your breakfast."

"But I had a feelin' in my bones you was gonna need me," Ruby said. "And it's past time I came back anyhow. Doc's as cantankerous as a bear with a sore head, and I told him he could get his own housekeeper."

"Someone should have woken me." Nathan's head spun with the notion that all this had gone on without his knowledge. "I could have—"

Done very little.

"Maybe fed the horses." He leaned against the kitchen worktable. "James can't handle everything on his own."

"Louis was done," Sally said. "He slipped coming down the ladder. But if Mrs. Buck is back, you won't be needing me, and with him unable to work . . ."

"Don't concern yourself about that, Sally." Nathan gave her a reassuring smile. "Ruby needs help around here still, and I'll keep paying his wages. He got hurt on my ladder after all. I should look at it and see if it needs to be replaced."

"I already done that, Dr. Nathan." James came through the back door, bringing the autumn smells of wood smoke and cold air with him. "I'm just going into town now to fetch our things."

"Then I'll go with you." Nathan's heart began to pound at

the imminent conversation. "When Dr. Maxwell comes back, tell her where I've gone."

If he harbored any doubts about the rightness of his actions, the memory of the night before, and the tentative restoration of camaraderie between Audrey and him, kept his resolve strong. He probably should have consulted a lawyer first, but he would worry about those kinds of details later.

He had plenty of time to plan the speech he would make to Doc, for the rain the day before had left the road slick with mud. James drove with care, taking longer than usual.

At last they arrived in town. Nathan alighted and, without assistance, climbed the steps to Doc's office.

He was seeing a patient. Which male voice belonged to the old doctor, Nathan couldn't tell. Both grumbled at bass level like distant thunder. Nathan grinned and sat down to wait.

Two more patients entered. Neither spoke to him, and he didn't recognize their voices. Newcomers. Many new people had moved into the Valley during the years he was away. To them he wasn't the local boy who'd gone to the city to make a name for himself. To them he was nobody.

Oddly, the idea no longer bothered him. What mattered was for him to matter to Audrey as more than the man who provided her with a roof over her head.

His plan, shaky though it was, should take him closer to his goal.

At last the office cleared and Doc invited him into the office. "For coffee." He was still grumbling. "Ruby took every whiskey bottle she could find and threw them out."

"And you can't afford to buy more?" Nathan probed with gentle teasing.

"I could. Been doing right well these last two or three months, thanks to you." Doc slipped a mug of hot coffee into Nathan's hands. "Good thing, since I'll have to hire a housekeeper now you stole Ruby back."

"Ruby came back on her own." Nathan sipped the coffee, grimaced at its bitterness, but maintained his hold on the cup. "I'm happy I could be of some assistance to you after neglecting my friends for so long."

Doc grunted. "You'd have been of more assistance if you'd come back here to practice instead of staying with those rich folk in the city. We needed you here all along and now . . . er . . . Well, this county needs two doctors. That midwife is next to useless."

"This county has two doctors." Nathan set his cup down on the table with a thud for emphasis. "Audrey is an excellent doctor. You should recognize that from what she did for my sister."

"She should have waited until I got there."

"Perhaps." Nathan resisted the urge to squirm. He had no defense for this one, as he hadn't examined Corinne himself and so could make no judgment on the urgency of the surgical delivery. "Audrey didn't think waiting was a good idea."

"Young doctors are always too quick to pull out a scalpel." Doc sipped his coffee. "Or don't you remember?"

"I don't remember being too quick to save someone's life when I thought it necessary." The familiar ache for his lost practice settled around Nathan's heart. He tried to dismiss it in favor of what he had to say and should have said weeks ago. "Nor do I recall a fellow practitioner being spiteful in front of others when I made a medical decision like that, whether he agreed with me or not."

"Spiteful, you say?" Doc scraped back his chair, crossed the room, and poured more coffee, clanging the metal coffeepot onto the stove. "Who was spiteful?"

With an effort, Nathan kept his tone neutral. "You know perfectly well you were when you told Audrey about what I said to the judge."

"Thought she had a right to know." Doc returned to the table.

"Should be no secrets between a man and wife. Never had them from my wife in fifty years."

"You may be right on that, but it wasn't your place to tell her."

Doc said nothing.

"I felt I needed to help you," Nathan plunged on. "You encouraged me to be a doctor and let me work with you before I got my training. I loved my work and owe you for that."

"This isn't about you working with me, is it?" Doc heaved a big sigh. "Nathan, you're a good man, and I appreciate all you've done for me, but . . . er . . ."

"It's not about that." Nathan filled in the awkward silence. "It's about Audrey. It's about showing my wife that I love her enough to give her the work she loves and wants."

"That has nothing to do with me." Doc's voice turned cold. "Your marriage is your concern."

"Yes." Nathan drummed his fingers on his thighs. "Doc, I haven't mentioned the money you owe her and, therefore, owe me. No, no, wait for me to finish. I have no intention of making you pay it, but it is a court order and . . . Well, if something happened to me, I know Audrey would insist on it."

"Nothing's going to happen to you."

"We always think that, don't we?" Nathan touched one of the scars on his temple. "But it can, so I want to clear the books, so to speak."

"No need. I plan to pay you within the month."

Nathan started. "You must be doing very well."

"Uh-huh."

Doc's near chuckle sent a frisson of uneasiness up Nathan's spine.

"Since maybe you should save that money for your retirement," he began slowly, "I want to offer to forgive the debt if you will set your resentment, or whatever it is, aside and let Audrey be your partner."

"Can't do it." Doc's chair scraped. "She might be a good

doctor—for a female, that is. Been hearing good things about her, and I admit she did well with Corinne. But—"

"Then why won't you even consider it? Life would be much easier if my old friend and my wife were colleagues, if not friends."

"Maybe so." Regret tinged Doc's voice. "Though she's not much good to me, expecting as she is."

"I suspect she'll still want to practice once the baby is born. She made a deathbed promise to do so to her first husband."

"I made one of those to my wife too." Doc cleared his throat. "Said I'd help you get back on your feet. But you did it without me and got me on mine instead."

"Then help me with this." Nathan didn't care if he was pleading.

Doc sighed. "I already said I can't. You see, now that I'm working regular again, I realized I'm getting too old to keep up this much work."

"Then a young partner is perfect."

"Yes, son, you're right. That's why I sold half the practice a month ago."

Chapter Fifteen

Audrey rubbed her aching back, then collapsed onto the dining room chair. As hungry as her stomach told her she was, as delicious as Ruby's cooking was certain to be, she doubted she possessed the energy to pick up her fork and dig into the fluffy potatoes and delicately roasted chicken.

She hated to admit it, but she was going to have to stop working. Even under full skirts and voluminous shawls, easy to justify in the chilly November weather, her increased girth had become too noticeable for her to be out in public much. And the fatigue. She simply wanted to lay her head on the table and sleep.

But she was striving.

A low groan escaped her lips before she could stifle it.

"Are you all right?" Nathan started to rise.

"Yes, thank you, I'm merely tired."

"No wonder." He narrowed his eyes. "Dare I suggest you stop working?"

Hairs stood up on the back of her neck. The tingle rippled down her spine, and she gripped the edge of the table, counting to ten. Something had been disturbing Nathan of late, and she didn't want to make matters worse between them. The rainy night they'd shared the fire and hot chocolate gave her hope matters would change between them. She must think he spoke out of concern, even medical concern, for her health and not because he wanted her to stop being a doctor.

"It frustrates me, but I admit you're probably right." She managed a smile, and some of her fatigue slipped away. "My condition is showing a bit too much too."

"Have you made a visit to the doctor or a midwife?" He began to eat as though the question were something whose answer wasn't all that important to him, but she saw the whiteness of his knuckles against his fork handle.

"The midwife is a fool." Audrey sliced off a mouthful of chicken and found it as succulent as she anticipated. "No, no, she's a good woman who can handle routine births, but she panics the moment something goes wrong."

"She isn't trained for more. That's why most women prefer doctors now." He gave her a mock ferocious scowl. "But you're avoiding my question."

She laughed. "So I am, because the answer is no. I won't go near Doc, and Winchester is so far away." She shrugged. "I'm a doctor. I know everything is all right. Good, in truth. Other than being tired, I've never felt better. It's probably Ruby's excellent cooking."

"You know you shouldn't make your own diagnosis. If I could—" He stopped his own words with a mouthful of string beans.

"At least you don't expect me to go to Doc." She grimaced.

"Of course not." He set down his fork. "Audrey, I need to tell you—"

A knock on the front door interrupted him.

"Who would call at this hour?" Audrey pushed back her

chair, hoping for the first time in her life it wasn't someone needing a doctor.

"Sit down. I'll get it." Nathan was already on his feet, striding to the door with so much confidence, one would think he could see except for the hand he held out a little in front of him.

Watching him, straight-backed and broad-shouldered, Audrey experienced an emptiness no amount of chicken or potatoes could fill. It had nothing to do with her stomach and everything to do with her heart.

If only he had something to do, matters could mend between them, she knew. Surely he only minded her practicing medicine because he couldn't. Now that she intended to stay home for a few months, perhaps he would stop distancing himself from her. Meanwhile she would keep looking through books and journals to find something he could do in the medical field. She knew she would hate losing the patients who would abandon her while she was unable to work.

She stamped down the bubble of resentment against the baby. She knew she must be an unnatural woman not to go all soft at the very thought of holding it. She knew she would love it once it was in her arms. For now, however, it felt like a burden holding her back and keeping her from what she loved most.

Even more than your husband?

She shoved that question aside for further examination and rose to find out what was taking Nathan so long.

The moment she crossed through the kitchen to the formal dining room they rarely used, she heard the voices. Women's voices. Familiar women's voices.

She leaned against the door frame and closed her eyes. Surely she was mistaken. Surely her fatigue was creating nightmares.

"This is precisely why we came." Her mother's voice broke over her like a sudden, icy rain shower. "She obviously needs someone to take care of her. What are you thinking, allowing her to gallivant around the countryside in her condition?"

"I'm thinking of her happiness." Nathan's firm but gentle tone was like the sunshine following the rain. "Forcing her to stay here with just me would certainly not achieve that."

"Her respectability is far more important than her happiness." Mrs. Sinclair seized Audrey's hands. "You should be in bed."

"No, I should be at the table finishing my dinner." Audrey looked at her mother, who was dressed in a dove-gray traveling suit and high, lace-collared blouse and frowning at her from beneath the brim of a gray felt hat. "What are you doing here, Mother? And Mrs. Vanderleyden?"

Adam's mousier mother stood behind Nathan. She, too, was dressed for travel, only her outfit was still the black of deep mourning.

"You're wearing crimson." Her eyes flashed accusation. "It's bad enough you dishonored my son by marrying within five months of his death, but to put off your blacks for crimson! I can't bear it."

Audrey suppressed the urge to respond, "If you hadn't foisted yourself upon us, you wouldn't have to."

Her good manners took over. "Have you eaten?"

"Yes, though a cup of tea won't go amiss," her mother said.

"I'll get it." Nathan seemed happy to find an excuse to slip into the kitchen and have something to do.

"Really, Audrey, should you let him?" Mrs. Sinclair started to follow Nathan into the kitchen.

Audrey grabbed her arm and stopped her. "Let him. He's capable."

"If Adam were here, he could have fetched us from the train." Mrs. Vanderleyden used a black-bordered handkerchief to dab her eyes, though they looked dry to Audrey. "But this man is nearly useless."

Audrey ground her teeth. "Nathan is far from useless. He's—" She gave up trying to persuade Mrs. Vanderleyden otherwise. "Adam wouldn't have known you were coming either. I suppose you expect to stay here?"

"Well, of course." Mother wrinkled her nose. "The house looks adequate."

It wasn't the twenty-room mansion she lived in or the seventy-one-room monstrosity of the Vanderleydens, but Audrey found the house cozy and better than adequate.

"We have four bedrooms. There would be six, and two dressing rooms, but Nathan's father liked the notion of bathrooms. I'll get Ruby to help me set up the extra rooms. You should be comfortable, though you'll have to share a bath."

"At least you have that much convenience." Her mother glanced around. "I thought you said you were eating."

"We are. In the breakfast room." Her stomach growling at the mention of the cooling food on her plate, Audrey spun on her heels and returned to the table.

Of course she couldn't stay there. Nathan needed rescuing in the kitchen before her mother demoralized him.

Nathan, however, merely smiled at Mrs. Sinclair's attempt to take over the tea making and stepped back from the stove. "If you like, I'll go join my wife and finish my dinner."

My wife sounded like music to Audrey's ears. Watching him walk toward her, she experienced an odd urge to hug him and thank him for referring to her that way.

Especially since you're not a very good one. "I'm sorry," she murmured instead.

"Why?" He grinned. "Did you invite them?"

"Goodness, no. I haven't even heard from either of them since I sent the telegram about our marriage."

"Nothing?"

She shook her head. "No. I got a short letter from my father. That's all."

"So why did they come?"

"We'll have to ask them." Audrey finished the last bite of

chicken on her plate and gathered the dishes to carry into the kitchen. "Why don't you go into your den. I'll manage the mothers."

"I'll go fetch Ruby to help set up beds."

"Oh, thank you. And perhaps get James to carry up their bags. It looks like they brought enough for . . ." She trailed off into a groan.

"A couple of months?" Nathan reached out his hand to her but stopped short of touching her hand.

She stood motionless, waiting to see if he would step forward and close the distance.

He turned his back to her and headed out the door.

Audrey sighed and carried the dishes to the kitchen sink. Her mother was just pouring steaming water over the leaves in a silver teapot.

"This is a fine set. Perhaps the Maxwells aren't really poor," she said.

"Nathan isn't poor at all." Audrey pumped water over the dishes but decided not to wash them.

"You don't have a maid, though." Mrs. Vanderleyden sounded appalled.

"We have Ruby and Sally during the day, or at night if we have guests." Audrey crossed to the kitchen door. "Since the two of you didn't bring a maid, I'll start getting your rooms ready."

"But we did bring a maid." Mrs. Vanderleyden looked pleased. "She's coming tomorrow with the rest of our luggage."

Audrey scanned the piles of bags cluttering the parlor floor and turned to stare at her mother and former mother-in-law. "You have more luggage coming? Are you moving in with me?"

"Only until after the baby comes," Mrs. Vanderleyden declared. "It belongs to me, after all, as the only remnant of my son."

"We'll leave sooner," Mrs. Sinclair added, "if you decide to come home with us."

"I have no intention of coming home with you." Audrey softened her demeanor. "I know you want me there, and I think it terribly kind of you, but my place is here."

"You may come back when my grandchild is born," Mrs. Vanderleyden assured her.

"But my husband is here." Audrey shook her head emphatically.

Yet Adam's mother was right. The grandchild was hers, not Nathan's child without any living grandparents. Perhaps the baby deserved to be raised in its rightful environment.

She really hadn't given her child enough thought because she'd been so caught up in her fight for her medical practice.

Conscience stabbed her on that point. At the same time, she had taken the vow to stay with Nathan.

And she had patients here. Even if she would have to stop working for a while, she would return, and they would expect her to. Many had said so, much to her gratification.

"And my work is here," she concluded her refusal.

"Not for long." Her mother's eyes shone with triumph. "While we were in town, we learned that Dr. Hornsby has taken on a partner."

"You knew." Audrey closed the door behind her with a decisive click. "You knew about Doc's new partner, but you didn't tell me."

"I knew." Nathan cradled a cup of tea between his cold fingers and wondered when the chill of apprehension would leave him. "I knew." He repeated the admission, not knowing how to proceed.

"Did you ever intend to tell me?" Her skirt rustled as she swept past him and settled in the other chair before the fire. He caught a whiff of her fragrance, all sweet springtime against the sharp spice of autumn, and his heart twisted.

He knew he deserved most of the censure in her words. His reasons for keeping his mouth shut would only make her angrier. And now that the mothers had arrived, encouraging her to leave, his dilemma grew stronger with the choices she now possessed, choices that would not benefit him no matter how he looked at it or what she decided.

"Perhaps I should ask why you didn't tell me." Hurt replaced the accusation in her tone.

"When I tell you, I think you'll understand." He stretched out his hand, reaching for hers.

She didn't accept the gesture.

He rested his palm on the plush arm of her chair. "This county is big enough for two doctors but probably not for three." He wished he were touching her so he could gauge her reaction to his words. "If Doc takes on this partner and keeps working too . . ."

"I can't stop working for months as I need to because of the baby." She sounded worn to a thread or maybe defeated. "All the work I've done to build my reputation will be lost. They'll need a doctor, and if I'm not available, they'll go to the man who will never be interrupted by childbirth."

"Some will wait for you to come back. . . . If they can."

"Expectant mothers can't wait. Sick children can't wait. A man with a broken leg can't wait. Oh, Nathan." Her voice broke. Her chair shifted, and suddenly she held his hand in both of hers. "I never understood, except in a small way, how you must have felt when you woke up and realized you could no longer practice." Her fingers tightened around his. "I'm only looking at the probability of it, and it hurts me to the core. How much worse for you."

"It wasn't easy. It still isn't." He slid off his chair and knelt on the floor beside hers. "Thanks to Corinne and her family, not to mention Ruby and James, I got through. They've been my encouragement to keep going. But to have nothing to do, nothing to contribute . . . But I do, and I've failed in my efforts to help you too."

"To help me?" She leaned forward, and a lock of her soft hair brushed his cheek. "Is that what Corinne meant when she said you had plans?"

"Partly. At first I asked Doc if I could work with him on difficult cases. Consult with him, use my knowledge as I did with you."

"And he turned you down?"

"Yes."

"Fool."

"I was probably the fool for asking." He made himself laugh it off. "Twice helping you wasn't enough to convince him I am capable."

"Why didn't you tell me?" The disapproval returned to her tone.

"I didn't want you to have any more reminders of my uselessness."

"Nathan, I—"

"So I tried something else." He rushed into speech before she could express words of sympathy, of which he had heard far too many in the past two years. "I tried to make another bargain with Doc. I told him if he would let you have half his practice when you're able to work after the baby, he wouldn't have to pay back the money."

"And he said no."

"He'd already sold part of the practice to this other doctor." Nathan raised one of her hands to his cheek. "I didn't know how else to convince you that I don't mind your practicing medicine."

"I-I don't know what to say." Her fingers trembled in his. "*Thank you* seems inadequate."

"And irrelevant, since I failed you. And now, if you don't

have a practice here . . . and with your mother and Mrs. Vander-leyden here . . ." He swallowed. "You don't need to stay."

"Of course I do." She brushed her fingers across his jaw, then removed her hand from his. "I'll have to stay so my patients will know that I haven't stopped working except when it's absolutely necessary."

Nathan flinched. First she caressed his face, then she might as well have kicked him in the belly when she said she stayed for her patients and not him.

He took care to moderate his tone. "Audrey, you can't keep working much longer. Besides the impropriety of it, you can't take risks with ice and snow. We don't get much here, and it doesn't last. But when we do, it comes on suddenly and can be fierce."

"For goodness' sake." Audrey surged to her feet and paced away from him, her footfalls solid, her skirt swishing like storm water against a lakeshore. "You know how it is to lose everything you've worked for. How can you expect me to give it up and let someone else take it over?"

"Because I care about your health and safety. They're not worth risking to hold on to a handful of patients."

"It won't be a thimbleful if I am unavailable for too long."

"And that thimbleful will be without the doctor they prefer if something happens to you." He rose, hands pressed against his thighs. "And where will I be without you?"

She said nothing but stopped pacing. He thought she looked at him.

"Yes," he said softly, "I want my wife and her baby. In the event you haven't taken note, family is important to me, probably more now than before. I left them once to pursue my career, but they didn't hold that against me. When I got hurt, they stood by me."

"Corinne, Russ, and the boys are wonderful." Audrey drew in an audible breath. "And so are you. I have worked so hard this past month to build up something important, to fulfill my promise to Adam. I don't know how I can just give it up."

"Even to protect his baby?"

"I won't risk the baby. That I can promise you. Now I must see if the mothers are settled." With a parting touch on his arm, she bustled from the room.

Nathan reached out in front of him and gripped the edges of the mantel. He knew as her husband he possessed the right to order her to stay home. He also knew that what tentative link held them together, a link other than the vows of marriage neither of them would break, he would shatter with that kind of governance. But he had no idea how to win her now. Every attempt slipped from his grasp.

Mastery of his own household seemed to slip from his grasp with every day the mothers stayed. Only his den remained off limits to them. He insisted on that, and Audrey stood by him. Apparently the older ladies respected a man's private territory and did not bother him there.

Yet that meant he saw less of Audrey than ever. Mrs. Sinclair insisted Audrey read to her and Mrs. Vanderleyden books in which Nathan had little interest. While Audrey read, the mothers knitted, stitched, and embroidered tiny garments. Nathan knew this because they drew him in to inspect each completed piece.

"Even if Audrey is an unnatural mother," Mrs. Vanderleyden declared, "no one at home will say my grandson is poorly dressed."

"But he or she won't live in Connecticut." Audrey pointed this out as often as necessary.

Mrs. Vanderleyden chattered on as though her former daughter-in-law hadn't spoken. "We will have to have a fine christening party. Perhaps that's when I will take off my blacks."

Impatient with the obvious assumption that Audrey would go back north with them, Nathan finally spoke up. "The christening will take place here. The child will be far too young to travel to Connecticut."

"That's why Audrey needs to come home with us." Mrs. Vanderleyden wasn't put off in the least. "The baby should be born in his future home."

"His or her future home is here," Audrey said.

"But he will be a Vanderleyden, not a Maxwell," Mrs. Sinclair pointed out.

"I am a Maxwell," Audrey said.

The four simple words cheered Nathan for days.

Until Corinne and Russell arrived for dinner a week later and announced that the new doctor had arrived.

"He's so young and handsome, half the unattached females in town have invented illnesses." Corinne laughed.

"He'd like to meet you, Nathan," Russell said. "He went to Johns Hopkins and has heard nothing but praise of your work."

"Sometime." Nathan remained noncommittal. As much as he would like to meet the newcomer, it stung him that the man hadn't asked to meet Audrey.

"You should pay Doc a visit too," Russell continued. "He's looking old. Two years of not taking care of his health has taken its toll on him, I think."

"He seemed well enough the last time I saw him." Nathan remained cautious.

"Russ thinks anyone who isn't as robust as he is, is sickly." Corinne turned her attention and charm to the mothers and Audrey. "You aren't still calling on patients, are you?"

While Nathan engaged with Russell in business talk, he listened to see if Audrey would admit to Corinne how much she had been working. Corinne expressed her disapproval more strongly than Nathan or the mothers had.

Disapproval made no difference to Audrey. She seemed driven by the need to be out of the house and working. At loose ends, Nathan was restless and annoyed enough to admit Audrey was right about one thing—he was jealous of her ability to work.

"But I never would have deliberately sabotaged your work," he said to himself. Telling her had done no good.

Nothing he suggested seemed to matter to her. Indeed, the more he tried to advise her to slow down and see a doctor in Winchester or perhaps even the new doctor in the county, the harder she seemed to work

The mothers weren't helping. They nagged her. That was the only word for the constant directives they gave on what she should eat and wear and whom she should befriend.

"I'm not surprised you insisted on education in Paris," Nathan admitted to Audrey one blustery December evening they found themselves alone.

"I went to Paris to get a superior education not yet available to females in this country, not to get away from my mother." She let out a rueful laugh. "I know they do it out of love and concern."

"I say what I do out of love and concern too." Nathan's heart pleaded for her to believe him.

Audrey sighed. "I wish—"

Pounding erupted on the front door.

"Who in the world?" Audrey's chair creaked.

"I'll get it." Nathan rose and headed for the door. The last chime of the clock had struck a quarter past ten. Knocking of this ferocity meant only one thing—a medical emergency.

"Surely you could go fetch one of the other doctors," Nathan grumbled under his voice.

He opened the door. A blast of snow-scented air swept in, stinging his face. "Yes?"

"It's my mother." The speaker was a youth. "It's her time."

"Can you get one of the other doctors—?"

"Of course he can't." Audrey bustled up beside Nathan. "I'll be right with you, Josh."

"Come in out of the cold." Nathan closed the door behind the boy, then followed Audrey up the stairs to her room. "You can't go out there. It's going to snow. You're only a month from your time, and you need your rest."

"She needs me, Nathan. She had a rough delivery last time."

"Who delivered her last one? The midwife?"

"No, Doc, but—"

"Then he can again. Audrey, you can't keep this up."

"I must. I must." Her voice sounded thick.

Nathan reached out to her, but she eluded him and left, her footfalls surprisingly swift and light for a lady in her condition.

Maybe she was in exceptional health. He could only hope. He couldn't make a judgment from her coloring or without examining her, and she wouldn't allow that.

All he could do was make himself coffee, sit up, and wait, then stew, make more coffee, and wait some more. He had started another carving, this time out of sandstone so he could use blunt tools. It made a mess, but neither Audrey nor Ruby complained.

"I'd rather clean up sand than blood," had been Ruby's only comment.

He thought maybe this carving would better resemble its intended shape than the wooden one had. Yet Audrey kept that misshapen dog on her bedside table. He knew this because he had overheard her mother saying she should put it in a drawer where the household help wouldn't see it.

"I should put it in the parlor for everyone to see." Audrey's response had made Nathan smile.

It gave him hope, and he smiled again now, until he heard the ping of sleet against the windows. Audrey shouldn't be out in this weather. He hoped she had reached her destination safely and intended to wait out the storm and not come home until morning.

But around two o'clock, the sound of horses' hooves

crunched up the drive at a pace far too fast for the weather or hour. Nathan headed out the front door and down the porch steps too fast for someone who couldn't see where he was going.

A horse whickered. The vehicle stopped. No one spoke. No one got down.

"Audrey?" Nathan reached the vehicle.

It was a low cart, the kind with only two wheels. Further inspection showed him a single horse stood between the shafts, its sides heaving, head drooping. It was the sort of cart a youth like the one who had collected Audrey would drive.

And the single seat was completely empty.

Chapter Sixteen

Audrey had never been colder in her life. Nor more frightened. Her clothes were soaked. Freezing rain kept pouring over her, and every time she moved, pain shot through her back and into her body. She lay on the four-mile stretch of road somewhere between the Gallagher farm and home.

And she was in labor.

"Noooo." She doubled over with the pain. "It's too soon."

It was too soon, but when a wheel of the cart slipped, she'd been thrown. A drift of sodden, molding leaves had broken her fall. Nothing had stopped the horse from galloping off.

It would head for the nearest horse stable it smelled. She needed to get up and walk the rest of the way home. Every time she tried to stand between bouts of pain, the combination of ice and wet leaves defeated her efforts. With nothing to grip for support, she simply could not rise.

Find a tree. She must find a tree. Perhaps a fence. Anything solid.

"Nathan." His name escaped from her lips in a feeble cry for help.

He was solid, strong in body and mind. If he were there, he could lift her, perhaps even carry her. He would ensure her warmth, her safety, the safety of her baby.

But he wasn't there because she lay on a road she never should have traveled in this weather. So much time had elapsed between her arrival and the appearance of the patient's baby, they could nearly have gone to Winchester and returned with a doctor. She'd been selfish and willful to the extent of foolishness.

Dangerous foolishness. Her obstinacy might cost her her life. Without help within an hour, probably less, it would cost the life of her baby.

"Oh, what have I done?"

She'd been trying to fulfill a promise to Adam. Yet Adam never would have expected her to fulfill that promise at the expense of his baby.

Especially when she was no longer certain it was her promise to Adam that drove her to take risks—risks that endangered her health and her baby's, risks that created a rift between her and the husband she loved.

"I've been so wrong. . . ."

She sobbed as she struggled to rise to her hands and knees.

Her girth and her skirts hampered her. Panting, sick with pain, she hunched inside her cloak and tried to look through the sleet and darkness for the nearest sturdy object.

The darkness was so intense, she could detect nothing close at hand. A sweep of each arm told her nothing lay within arm's length. She didn't even know in which direction she should crawl. If she ended up in the road, she would have farther to go and perhaps be in the way of any vehicles traveling at that time of night. Doubtful though that might be, it presented further danger. Moving in the other direction could lead her to an open field and make it more difficult to find her. If anyone could find her.

Nathan would expect her to stay at the Gallaghers' all night. She should have. But she'd wanted to get home. Even with the mothers there, home was comfort and serenity and feeling warm beside a fire with Nathan.

How she yearned to be beside a fire with Nathan, talking about anything from poetry to medicine, politics to farming.

They were friends.

They could be more.

They could have been more. If she didn't get to shelter soon, Nathan would be a widower without having ever truly had a wife.

"I don't know how we can go huntin' anyone, Dr. Nathan." James' teeth chattered in counterpoint to the drumming rain. "No tellin' where we'll end up ourselves."

"But people will know where we are." Nathan could not think of any alternative to heading out in complete darkness. "I have to go," Nathan concluded.

"Dr. Nathan, you'll freeze too." James grasped his arm. "You can't just go wandering off."

"Wouldn't you take the risk if it were Ruby?"

"Yes, sir, but I can—" James broke off in a fit of coughing.

Nathan understood the end of the sentence. James had been about to tell him he could see.

For thirty-four years Nathan had been told he could do anything he pleased. For the past two years he'd been told he couldn't do anything at all. Yet he'd learned to stoke the stove and make coffee. He was able to take care of himself and could even carve after a fashion. Hunting in the sleet for his wife might be a stretch from conquering the path between the house and the barn, but that had seemed insurmountable at one time too.

"I'm going." As a concession to good sense and safety he added, "Let's find the longest rope we have."

If nothing else helped them keep their way, each would at

least know where the other was with the ends of the line tied around their waists with thirty feet between them. Moments before they set out, Mrs. Sinclair dashed to hand Nathan a walking stick and James an umbrella.

"These will help you stay upright, and you can feel around along the side of the road," she explained. "If she was the one driving, she won't be far from the road, I'm sure."

A quaver in her voice suggested she was anything but certain.

"If she's all right and my grandson isn't . . ." Mrs. Vanderleyden's voice drifted out from the house.

She never finished the implied threat. Nathan doubted she could. In the past twenty minutes, he'd reached the conclusion that the mothers adored Audrey, even if they didn't approve of her choices in life and were frantic with worry.

Their bossiness and worry helped steady him and suppress the what-ifs shuddering through him.

Already cold, Nathan headed out along the drive, encouraged by the tautness of the rope yet knowing he was on his own. He could do this. He had to do this. His wife, his heart, depended on his success.

Success seemed as unattainable now as it had when he was a medical student. With no sight and only limited hearing due to the noise of the ice storm, he moved far too slowly. Poking and prodding the stick around himself, he stirred up shrubbery, rock breaks, and broken branches. No Audrey. No one at all. He lost count of how many times he slipped on patches of ice or James gave an exclamation when he came close to falling.

As they left the drive and headed onto the road, a breaking branch sent a crack echoing through the night like a gunshot. Nathan started, slid on ice-packed gravel, and went down on one knee. Pain shot up his leg. Digging the walking stick into the thawed earth of the packed ground, he started to rise.

He caught a whiff of springtime in the sharpness of approaching winter.

"Audrey?" He was mad. For him to smell her fragrance, she would have to be close. If she were that close, she could have gotten herself home.

Unless she were too badly injured to move.

Injured or . . . worse.

"Audrey?" he called more loudly.

"D'you find her?" James called.

"I don't know." Nathan began to crawl through the slush and drifted leaves, reaching, patting, sniffing. "Audrey, speak to me."

A groan sounded above the splash of the rain.

Nathan stood still, listening for the sound to repeat itself. A groan meant she was alive and conscious.

Another branch cracked, and he realized the moan had been the wind through an ice-laden branch about to break.

Sick with disappointment, he kept hunting, sweeping the stick around in a wider arc. James joined him, and they crept through the frozen mulch at the edge of the field, calling her name and waiting for a response.

Another groan sounded. Conscious that if an ice-burdened branch landed on his head, it could crack his skull, Nathan raised his arms for protection. But no gunshotlike sound was heard.

"Audrey, was that you?" He listened so hard for a rustle or a whisper of breath, he felt as though his ears stood out on either side of his head. His nostrils flared. Over the spice of the leaves and tang of the rain, again he caught a whiff of sweet lilies.

"She's here," Nathan announced. "I can smell her."

James let out a dubious snort, but his thrashing around told the tale that he was still looking.

"Audrey." Nathan spoke softly. "Make a noise again. We'll find you."

A sound a little louder than a heavy sigh rippled through the rain. It was enough for Nathan to move in her direction and find her.

Ice coated her cloak, her hair, and her skirt. She shivered so violently, he could scarcely get his arms around her. And when he did, he felt the spasm, and his training told him what was going to happen all too soon.

"James, lead me back to the house. I'll carry her."

"But, Doctor—"

"No time to argue."

Protesting all the way, James used the rope to guide Nathan back to the house while Nathan cradled Audrey in his arms. Several times she tried to speak, but her chattering teeth made the words unintelligible.

"Wait until you're warm." He made his voice calm, soothing, not at all reflective of what he felt inside.

When they reached the front steps, the door flew open, emitting warm air into the frigid night.

"My baby," Mrs. Sinclair cried. "Is she . . . all right?"

"She's in labor." Nathan didn't stop at the threshold. He knew his own house well. Carrying his precious burden, he headed up the steps, issuing orders all the way. "Warm blankets and hot bricks. James, fetch the doctor. The young one. Be careful, but hurry."

The mothers listened to him. In moments, they had Audrey in dry garments and tucked into bed. She didn't try to speak again, though moans emanated from her in intervals far too close together for Nathan's comfort.

"Is my grandson going to die?" Mrs. Vanderleyden asked tearfully. "He's early."

"Only a month. That's usually all right." Nathan gripped Audrey's hand, letting her squeeze as hard as she needed to through the contractions. "She'll be fine."

He hoped.

"Not if the baby comes before the doctor gets here." Mrs. Sinclair made no effort to disguise her weeping. "Oh, the foolish girl, why won't she listen to anyone?"

"She made a promise to her husband." The words ripped from Nathan. "She's been afraid of breaking it."

Audrey made a noise and tugged on his hand.

He leaned toward her. "What is it, my . . . love?"

"Wrong." She gasped for breath. "I was . . . wrong. Promise only . . . excuse . . . own way."

"Shh." He brushed hair away from her brow. "That's not important now."

"Yes. Yes, it is." Her voice grew stronger. "I've been thoughtless. Selfish . . . Help me. You've got to help me."

"I'm right here." He couldn't help her any other way.

"No, no, the baby." Audrey's groan sounded like that of a huge tree under the weight of its limbs. "It's coming."

"But I can't—"

"Why not?" Impatience rang through her voice. "Doctor . . . can't see . . . anyway . . . Please." The anguish in the last word sent him jumping to his feet and examining her, knowing that Audrey—woman, mother, physician—knew what she was talking about.

She always knew he could do this. She'd encouraged him, found ways for him to manage, and let him stumble and fall and make mistakes so he could keep going.

She believed in him, and because of that, he could help her.

Audrey leaned back against a pile of fresh pillows, her daughter nestled in her arms. She had known she would love the baby once it arrived but hadn't been prepared for the wave of tenderness turning her bones into a puddle of warmth and joy. With her daughter small but safely delivered, Audrey forgot about the hour in the dark and ice.

She would never forget the exhilaration of hearing Nathan's

voice calling her name. She'd been about to lose consciousness. His voice brought her back.

His voice, the words he spoke, his whole presence would always bring her back from whatever brink her foolishness might incline her to tip over.

She smiled, her heart overflowing. "You did great work, Dr. Maxwell."

"I think you did most of the work." He caressed her cheek, and his smile glowed like sunshine in the deep gray of dawn. "Would you like to sleep now?"

"Do I have to let go of—what will we call her?"

"Drusilla," Mother Vanderleyden answered first. "The first daughter is always named for her paternal grandmother. She's Drusilla Vanderleyden."

"That's a big name for something so tiny." Audrey gazed at the tiny mouth, the perfect fingers.

Yes, she was wrinkled and red with the misshapen head of a newborn, but Audrey had never seen anything more beautiful.

"We can decide—"

A clatter in the drive followed by the thud of the front door heralded someone's arrival.

"Which way do I go?" The question came from a stranger.

Audrey stiffened, and the baby began to mewl. From the corner of her eye, Audrey saw Nathan stiffen.

"The doctor, I presume." His smile had faded.

"You're too late." Mrs. Sinclair went to the bedroom door. "She's already delivered."

Swift footfalls pounded on the steps. A moment later, a young man with bright hazel eyes and a shock of dark hair spilling over his brow charged into the room. "So sorry I didn't get here on time. Terrible weather. How are you, Mrs. Maxwell?"

"Dr. Maxwell," Nathan said. "And I'm Mister—"

"He's Dr. Maxwell too." Despite her aches and pains and

mind-numbing fatigue, Audrey wanted to laugh at the young doctor's befuddled expression.

"I'm . . . er . . . Jason Trilby. And since I'm here, shall I examine the . . . er . . . mother? Many complications can occur after if—"

"I had perfectly competent care, Dr. Trilby." Audrey could barely keep her smile from widening. "Dr. Nathan Maxwell is a fine physician and midwife."

"But—oh, my." Trilby's eyes grew even brighter, and he strode forward to pump Nathan's hand. "Sir, it's an honor to meet you. You're practically a legend in Baltimore."

"True," Nathan murmured dryly. "They expected me to die from that gunshot."

"Oh, that, no. I was referring to your medical knowledge. I mean, if you attended to the lady, I expect she is all right."

"Well, um . . ." Color washed up Nathan's face. "I did my best."

"He did well," Mother concurred. "I've seen many lyings-in, and he did well."

"My granddaughter is safe, and that matters to me," Mrs. Vanderleyden added.

The talk and the praise continued around Audrey. Voices grew distant and foggy. She felt someone remove the baby from her arms and recalled protesting yet not too hard. She couldn't stay awake a moment longer.

What felt like a moment later, she awoke to the soft mewling cries of her baby. She struggled to sit up, but before her eyes were fully open, Ruby set the child in her arms.

"I'll get Dr. Nathan." She swept from the room.

Moments later Nathan came in, his face bright and his steps light for a man with circles under his eyes.

"Did you sleep at all?" Audrey asked.

"No. Trilby and I have been talking and drinking too much coffee. The weather's too bad for him to travel yet."

"I suppose I don't need to ask if Ruby fed you." Her own stomach growled at the prospect of food.

"More than we needed." Nathan laughed. "Are you hungry?"

"Yes, but let me hold her until she sleeps again. What did you talk about?"

"He's worried about Doc."

Audrey ground her teeth.

"He's encouraging him to retire except for emergencies." Nathan settled onto the chair. "Two years of not taking care of himself have taken their toll. He is over seventy."

"So will he bring someone else new in?" Audrey yawned.

"Yes." Nathan turned his face away. "He asked me if I'd work with him. I hope you don't mind."

"Mind? Nathan, I've never heard anything so wonderful. How . . . I don't mean to sound rude, but how does he think you can help?"

"I could consult and . . . He's quite sure I could deliver babies. Not many doctors see what they're doing anyway, and he's read about a blind doctor in England who does well. . . ."

His voice trailed off, and Audrey waited for the pain, the stab of betrayal, the annoyance at the thought that Trilby had asked Nathan and not her. Instead, she experienced more glowing warmth inside.

"You accepted, of course," she said.

"I didn't want to accept without talking to you first." His lashes half covered his eyes. "For two years, I've been told I can't do things. They said I couldn't find you. But I did. And I've done more I've been told I can't. In my heart, I've known what I can do—or think I can do—but I've been afraid I'd fail and make a fool of myself. But being around you, seeing you work and work and work to keep what you've fought for . . ." He shrugged and began to drum his fingers on his thighs. "There is a lot I can't do anymore. But not as much as I used to think."

"So you want to accept?" She stared down at her baby, reminded of how close she had come to losing this precious scrap of life, knowing now what she had to do.

"Yes, I want to." Nathan reached out and rested his hand on her shoulder. "But not if it will continue to create this rift between us. Assuring you that you come first in my life, that I love you more than my need to work, is . . . well, of the utmost importance."

"Nathan." Tears closed her throat. Her hands full with her child, she bent her head to capture Nathan's hand between her cheek and her shoulder while she regained enough composure to speak. "I don't need proof that you love me. You've been nothing but loving to me from the beginning. That you would give up your chance to work again to spare my feelings . . ." Tears spilled from her eyes and onto his hand.

The baby woke and began to cry.

"It's all right, little one," Nathan purred. "We're all right."

She stopped in mid-whimper.

"Amazing." Audrey gazed up at him in awe. "She likes your voice."

"I hope she likes me." He stroked the baby's cheek with one finger. "I figure I can help take care of her when you're with patients."

"If there are any for me." Audrey took a deep breath. "I've been wrong. I kept telling myself I was working to fulfill my promise to Adam. It was true, but not for selfless reasons. I-I did it out of guilt. He sacrificed a great deal so I could get a medical education, including having a loving wife who would bring him his slippers and not leave him in the middle of the night. I thought I should work hard to make up for that deficiency in myself. But in the end I endangered the baby he badly wanted, and I hurt you. I put my work before everyone, including myself. I let practicing medicine hold me away from—from loving my baby and from loving you. I can't let that happen again."

He looked completely shocked. "Audrey, you're not giving up medicine."

"Oh, no, I don't think I could ever do that." She let out a tiny laugh, as a bigger one would hurt. "I haven't grown that self-sacrificing overnight. But if we could work together . . . There are a few husband-and-wife doctor teams. I could help you, and perhaps"—she let a teasing note into her tone—"you could bring yourself to help some with the children."

"Children?" His face took on its earlier glow. "You want children?"

"More children." She smiled at her now sleeping daughter. "One isn't nearly enough."

"But she's—"

"We've brought you breakfast." Mrs. Sinclair bustled into the room bearing a tray of dishes.

Mrs. Vanderleyden followed with a teapot. "How is the baby doing? Have you named her yet?"

"Not yet," Audrey admitted, "but I have a suggestion."

"What's that?" the older ladies chorused.

Nathan merely raised his eyebrows.

"The name Stephen is popular in the Vanderleyden family." Audrey smiled as she mentioned her first husband's middle name, knowing Nathan would hear the love in her voice even if he could not see it on her face. "So I will call her Stephanie Maxwell . . . for both of her fathers."